PENGUIN BOOKS

1806

SEPTEMBER ROSES

ANDRÉ MAUROIS

André Maurois

SEPTEMBER ROSES

Translated by Gerard Hopkins

*

PENGUIN BOOKS
IN ASSOCIATION WITH
THE BODLEY HEAD

Penguin Books Ltd, Harmondsworth, Middlesex
AUSTRALIA: Penguin Books Pty Ltd, 762 Whitehorse Road,
Mitcham, Victoria

—

Les Roses de septembre first published 1956
This translation first published by The Bodley Head 1958
Published in Penguin Books 1962

—

Copyright © Gerard Hopkins, 1958

—

Made and printed in Great Britain
by C. Nicholls & Company Ltd
Set in Linotype Juliana

This book is sold subject to the condition
that it shall not, by way of trade, be lent,
re-sold, hired out, or otherwise disposed
of without the publisher's consent,
in any form of binding or cover
other than that in which
it is published

FOR SIMONE

PART ONE

There are many ways of telling the truth without telling it completely! Can detachment be ever so complete as not to admit of an occasional backward glance at matters one has disavowed? What heart can be so sure of itself as to guarantee that no feeling of regret will slip between resignation, which depends upon ourselves, and forgetfulness which can come only with time?

EUGÈNE FROMENTIN

I

THE evening was mild and misty. In the pathways of the Bois a carpet of dead leaves creaked beneath the feet with a muffled, silky sound. How unexpected an air of youthfulness, thought Hervé Marcenat, did the rapidity of his movements, the slimness of his figure, and the brightness of his eyes, give to the man walking beside him. He tried to make him talk about his books.

Fontane stopped dead, raised his stick to point at the sky, and said, indignantly:

'No, no, my friend! let us leave those wretched works of mine in peace. You may think it affectation on my part, but I assure you that I have almost forgotten them. What could be more natural? A book is – what? – the hardening, the fixing, of a moment's thought. ... The author takes a – hm – mould of his passions at a specific instant of time which we may call M^i. But the man you meet ten, twenty years later belongs to both M^i and M^{ii}: he has no longer anything in common with the author of the book you love other than a few memories of childhood. The Guillaume Fontane who once sat in a shabby room, writing those *Exercises* which you are kind enough to praise so highly, is to me, now, almost a stranger. That is why a writer feels profoundly indifferent to his early work, and intolerably bored if he finds himself compelled to re-read it. That experience will be yours in good time.'

'And yet, *cher maître*, Balzac loved to discuss his heroes.'

'Balzac was that rarest of all phenomena – a true novelist. I am no more a novelist than was Montesquieu, and he was scarcely one at all.'

9

'But, your novels – '

'My friend, when you come to know me better you will understand how my novels came to be born. I expect you have heard tell of those ardent and foolish women who, when they have met a man whom they admire, say to him: "I should so like to have a child by you! ... " Imagine, instead, that some woman once said to me, "I should so like to have novels from you" ... and you won't be so very far from the truth. I gave way – one always does give way. The part of Joseph is a humiliating one to play. I have, therefore, been more than once – hm – guilty of sin, and my novels were the offspring of those moments of weakness. But I can't say that those brief "affairs" mean very much to me now.'

'What, then, *does* mean much to you?'

'*Very* much?'

Guillaume brandished his stick at the clouds.

'I'll tell you. First and foremost the pleasure of thinking: not, mark you, for the purpose of writing down my thoughts, but simply for my own enjoyment, when I read the thinkers. What really matters to me? Dawdling in a library, opening, here and there, a book at random, finding, as I idly turn a page, some phrase which suddenly enchants me; re-reading an author who was once the companion of my youth; discovering that my emotion is still new and intact. What really matters to me? Friendship, when it springs from mutual esteem, when it sounds the harmony struck from twin sensibilities – above all, when that friendship exists between a man and a woman and derives a certain degree of warmth from sensuality without – hm – being burned to a cinder by jealousy.'

'Then, you do not love your work?'

'Indeed, I do – or, let us say that I *should* love my work were it to consist in begetting, after years of laborious idleness, one short masterpiece – *Candide* or *Les Fleurs du mal*. I should dearly love slowly to accumulate a collection of Maxims and Characters. We all of us write too much. It is not that we want to, but that we are compelled to – after all, a man has got to live. Since you, dear friend, are just starting on your career as a writer – it is the fashion, nowadays, to call it a career – let me give you a few personal provisional rules of literary morality. You won't act on them – I don't myself – but that does not make them the less excellent. Do not live in Paris. Visit it from time to time to observe those social phenomena which you have to know about, but do your work in some place where you can be sure of solitude. Never meet a publisher nor an editor. Correspond with them, if you have to, but take notice neither of their approaches nor of their advice. Never bother about the market-value of a book. Boileau *gave* his books to Claude Barbin; he didn't sell them, and, though he said of Racine:

> *Je sais qu'un noble esprit peut, sans honte et sans crime*
> *Tirer de son travail un tribut légitime ...*

that was – hm – the indulgence of a friend who, in his heart of hearts, disapproved. ... On no account let yourself be swayed by the advice of a wife, a mistress, or a flatterer. Publish little: don't open your hand until it is full. Above all, concentrate on *form* – *form*, my dear friend, *form*, because only form will give a lasting quality to an author's work. Subject does not matter: Theocritus noted down the talk of a few housewives; Cicero pleaded dull administrative cases; Pascal carried on with Jesuits, who were really the product of his own imagination, a controversy which, today, is as dead as mutton. If these men are still read, centuries after they left this earth, it is because of their strict regard for form. That alone can

11

enable a man to leave his mark on life. It is better to write a poem than a novel. Oh! I am well aware that I have written novels which are very far from poems, but I have no affection for them; I should like you to know that. *Video meliora proboque.*'

He had delivered this tirade with passion, jabbing at the gravel of the path with his stick.

'How severe you are on yourself!' said Hervé. 'Your novels are full of poetry: as to your form, I prefer its unadorned simplicity to all the tricky writing of some I could name, where each word seems to glitter with an isolated brilliance.'

They had reached the Porte Saint-James. Fontane stopped between the gates, took up a solid stance facing his young companion, and barely escaped being knocked down by a car which was entering the Bois.

'Nonsense!' he said. 'Allow me at least the privilege of knowing my own limitations!'

'But if that is how you feel, *cher maître*, why not seek to please yourself? You are a free man, famous enough and rich enough not to have to depend on anybody. Why don't you live as you want to live?'

'My excellent friend,' said Fontane, 'you know nothing of life. She is a slut with a will of iron. She'll get the better of you, as she has of others, and don't run away with the idea that I am a rich man – very far from it. True, I did marry a rich wife, but the war has knocked all that sideways, and, as a result of the devaluation of the franc, Pauline is now a poor woman. But she still has the tastes of a rich one, and, in order to enable her to live in the style to which she has become accustomed, I have been forced to prostitute myself. Here we are – let us cross the road.'

Fontane's Neuilly home stood in a garden at the junction of the Boulevard Richard Wallace and the rue de la

Ferme. It was a pretentious villa with mullioned windows adorned with twisted balconies, and was flanked by a terrace with a scrolled balustrade – a mixture of sham Gothic and sham Renaissance, dating only too clearly from the nineteen hundreds. Fontane led his companion into the garden, which, like that of a provincial Prefecture, was planted with oval beds of violet and yellow pansies. He pointed his stick, disgustedly, at the façade.

'Just look at it!' he said. 'Is that where a writer should live – a place stinking of money, and, not to put too fine a point on it, perfectly hideous? I should have settled down either in a place of beauty or in a cell. But how? My wife inherited this ... this monstrosity from her first husband. It is always difficult, if not impossible, to break with the past. ... Come in for a moment, and I will show you the Keep, the core of the defences; one has, you see, to organize a protective system.'

He showed Hervé into a pillared vestibule with a black-and-white marble floor, like the entrance-hall of an hotel, then down a few steps into the library. Luxurious bindings filled unbroken rows of shelves where the light picked out stray points of gold. Fontane looked round the room.

'Here, at least,' he said, 'I am my own master. Sit down, my friend.'

There was a discreet knock at the door, and an elderly man, wearing a white jacket, came in. He was fat, pompous, and glib, and had the unctuous voice and smooth manners of a stage cleric.

'Madame has asked me to remind you, sir, that you are dining at the Embassy, that it is already half past seven, and that white tie and tails will be worn.'

Guillaume Fontane sighed, raised his eyes to the ceiling, and turned to his guest:

'White tie!' he said: 'That is the extent to which I

13

am my own master. A tail-coat, the livery of servitude!
Oh well ... but you need not move for another five
minutes. Alexis, tell your mistress that in here I am at
the service of the Muses, and that if I leave this room, it
will be only from force of habit.'

Alexis, with a greasy and indulgent smile, moved
softly to the door, and Fontane turned again to Marcenat.

'Devil take all embassies!' he said; 'unpunctuality is
the politeness of artists. Make no mistake about that.
The artist pleases as much by reason of his revolt against
the conventions as by his work. He should be the very
incarnation of liberty. The bourgeois thinks, with assumed anger, "Those chaps Verlaine and Rimbaud got
away with a lot of things!" – but in his heart of hearts
he's as pleased as Punch to think that they did. Take that
chap, for instance, the chap who makes motor-cars, who's
always asking me to dinner, what *is* his name? – you
know – that's where we met –'

'Larivière?'

'That's it, Larivière. Well, he's grateful to me for still
being late, unreliable, and a dawdler, in spite of social
and domestic duties, because that's what he'd like to
be, but hasn't the courage. "*Your work!*" says my poor
wife, in tones of awe. Work! the Sanctity of work!
"Thou shalt earn thy bread by writing novels," said the
Lord. Why, I ask you? What if the Puritans were
wrong? What if life was made, not for work but for
pleasure? The Puritan makes a fortune by turning his
back on pleasure, but he doesn't get any fun out of his
fortune! The whole thing is based on false premises.
"Vanity of vanities, all is vanity", said Ecclesiastes, but
didn't believe a word of it! Read him again and you'll
see that Ecclesiastes was an old lecher who, when the
change of life found him out, consoled himself with
lamentations!'

He talked on in this way for a good half-hour, and surrendered at last only at the third summons, which Madame Fontane delivered in person. Wearing full evening-dress, she looked, with her bare, firm-fleshed shoulders and a diamond crescent in her hair, every inch the Great Lady. Those 'velvety eyes' of which, once upon a time, the social columns of the papers had been so full still had their fascinating brilliance. Her obvious intelligence attracted strangers; her imposing *gaucherie* kept them at a distance. She made one think of those shy sovereigns who unconsciously antagonize their subjects. She gave Hervé a hostile look.

'I implore you, sir, to let my husband get dressed. We ought to be on our way already. Really, Guillaume, do show a little common sense !'

'Pauline,' said Fontane, 'please do not introduce common sense into matters which have no room for it. Well, my friend, good night – and come again soon.'

'Yes, indeed,' said Madame Fontane. 'You must lunch with us one day. That will be the best way of seeing Guillaume without interrupting his work.'

Outside, the moon, already riding high, was making a pattern of short, hard-edged shadows. Pallid street-lamps showed at intervals along the deserted, interminable, and melancholy boulevard. On his way to a distant Métro station, Marcenat wondered what lay behind Fontane's bitter jesting. Mounting revolt? or garrulous resignation? What sort of a woman was Pauline Fontane? – valued adviser, or domestic tyrant? He did not know the answers, and was astonished to find himself thrown so rapidly into an intimate relationship with a man he had always thought of as being inaccessible.

2

EDMÉE LARIVIÈRE lived in a perfect flat in a dilapidated house on the Quai de Béthune. Hervé Marcenat, who had already been waiting twenty minutes for her to come in, noted that the pictures, with their crude colours and aggressively angular lines, had been deliberately arranged so as to clash with the high Louis XV panelling and the white Chinese vases. Red amoebae, between the windows with their old brocade curtains, flanked a banner-blue, grooved cylinder set at a slant. He got up to examine in greater detail the books on the shelves, and found in them the same general bitter-sweet flavour.

'My cousin Edmée', he thought, 'is a sensitive and complicated woman.'

The tall young man, but recently arrived from the Limousin, was entirely lacking in the abrupt and off-hand manners of his contemporaries. He found a great deal more pleasure in understanding people than in condemning them.

The curved door opened, and Edmée came in. She was wearing a light-grey suit of superb simplicity. Though forty, she still retained the appearance of a young girl. Her fresh and smooth complexion seemed to be the outward and visible sign of a temperament at peace with itself. Hervé delighted in the pure modelling, the chamois eyes, the voice, and the clear-cut ideas of his cousin, though her angelic severity always made him feel slightly uneasy.

'Sorry, Hervé; I'm a bit late.'

'Not very: I was admiring your pictures.'

'That Vlaminck's pretty good, don't you think? How are things going? Signed your press-copies yet?'

She regarded herself as the protectress and suzerain of the country cousin who was just about to make his début in the world of Paris.

'Yes, I'm through with them: but the wording's given me a bit of a headache.'

'Don't let that worry you: nobody reads the inscriptions. Had many letters?'

'Only one: but I was as pleased as Punch to get it – from Guillaume Fontane.'

'Guillaume's actually written?'

'Indeed he has – and his letter has gone to my head.'

'What a flatterer! Our Guillaume is not prodigal of his prose. Do you admire him? I should have thought that your generation would have broken away from his influence.'

'Affinity would be a truer word than admiration. I know his weaknesses, and I like them.'

'Have you met him?'

'Indeed I have: I've been for a walk with him in the Bois. I even went home with him.'

'And I expect his wife turned you out in next to no time?'

'Not exactly: but she does seem to keep a tight hold on him. Tell me about her, Edmée.'

She seemed to be collecting her thoughts. 'Pauline Fontane?' she said, after a while. 'I have known her for a long time. She used to visit my parents when I was a little girl. In those days she was Madame Boersch, the wife of a banker who provided the financial backing for father's publishing business. Lovely to look at, powerful, domineering. What do you want to know about her? Her maiden-name was Pauline Langlois, and she came of a University family. Her father was Rector at Nancy – a philosopher. Father brought out his *Vocabulaire philosophique*. She grew up in a world of professors. She was a cultivated young woman, as those say who aren't – or, at least, very well informed.'

'And why did she marry a banker?'

'Why not? – after all, I married a motor manufacturer. I don't really know much about the Boersch set-up. It all happened at Nancy. Boersch was a good deal older than her, and in a position to offer what almost amounted to Royal Status. The Langlois family must have brought a good deal of pressure to bear, and Pauline, who was very ambitious, gave way. ... As it turned out, Boersch had the decency to die shortly after the marriage, and left his widow of twenty-two a house in Nancy, another at Neuilly (in which the Fontanes now live), an estate in Lorraine, and a fortune which she has used in the service of literature – or, rather, of those who follow the literary profession.'

'How did she get to know Fontane?'

'She entertained a great many writers. I suppose they provided her with some sort of "compensation". After all, as the daughter of a Rector, she must have looked on her marriage with a businessman as something of a come-down. She had been credited, perhaps wrongly, with a number of "literary affairs", which became increasingly notorious. Then Guillaume Fontane came on the scene, and his brilliance threw all the others into the shade. She had discovered him, and that, for her, was a matter of great pride. At first she clung to him because she believed in his future. Love came later, but when it came it filled her life. That is what makes her such a sympathetic person. But I warn you! – her jealousy is something to beware of. Still, no doubt about it, she it was who created the Fontane we know.'

'Created? Isn't that a slight exaggeration, Edmée? Fontane needed nobody to "create" him. His talent dated from long before he met her.'

'What a very simple young man you are! Talent and fame are two very different things. Sometimes they coincide, but quite often they remain separate. There are certain darlings of fortune who can't write – "*the sky looks threatening today; I shall put on my warm underclothing*" – without being hailed as geniuses, while others, who really have genius, are never recognized until they are dead.'

'That is true, but the reason is – they did not wish for fame. Stendhal preferred getting excited over Métilde, or gossiping with Mérimée, to pontificating on official occasions. Everyone gets what he wants.'

'Precisely. Guillaume, in his pre-Paulinian period, deliberately turned his back on success. He led an obscure life dedicated to the search for happiness, which, in his case, was a combination of sensuality, idleness, and reading. You've only to look at the dates to realize that Guillaume is fifty-eight. What did anyone know of him twenty years ago? The *Dialogues* and the *Exercises* were generally regarded as "difficult". Then, suddenly, the rhythm of his production took on a quicker beat, and he started to turn out a volume or two every year. One after the other, he was awarded the rosette of the Legion, the Collar, and an Oxford doctorate. He can be a member of the Academy whenever Pauline wishes; but she wants the Nobel Prize first, and that, too, he'll get. Why all this deluge of honours? Fontane was still the same Fontane, but Pauline was wielding the conductor's baton.'

'How do you mean?'

'She set the imponderables moving, persuaded the critics to strengthen their adjectives a bit, induced Fame

19

to sound a new note on her trumpet – *genius* instead of *talent*. She whipped the professors to heel, for the prestige of her family still counted with them. She unleashed the Sorbonne; she cultivated the foreigners. She made her weak but illustrious husband write articles, and travel here, there, and everywhere. In that way, by easy stages, she turned his Muse into a star performer.'

'You are cruel, Edmée, for all your sweet and solemn airs: unfair, too, because Fontane has never descended to vulgarity. It wasn't he who wooed the public, but the public that came to him.'

'Of course. Don't put words into my mouth. Our Guillaume has never been a fool: he wouldn't know how. But there is something lacking in what he is writing now – mystery, tremolo. His novels, you'll say, are well constructed. Maybe: but do they thrill us as the *Exercises* did? I don't think so. Not that Pauline has a mediocre mind. I have had many letters from her. They are amusing, carefully composed, neatly phrased. And that's not all. What she feels for Guillaume is something more than mere devotion. It is, I should say, closer to worship. But, to my mind, she has mistaken her husband's true interests. She is forcing him to sacrifice – how shall I put it? – real depth to surface brilliance. But that is not the way in which Guillaume's mind works. He is beginning to feel that her influence is distorting him, divorcing him from his true self; and, occasionally, he kicks over the traces. There may be danger in that, for her.'

'You may be right. The other day, when I was with him in his library, she started nagging him about some dinner or other, and I got the feeling that he was a bit restive.'

A look of satisfaction slowly showed on Edmée's face.

'That's all to the good; bravo, Guillaume! You see, we

women, with our demands and our moods, can so easily push a man to a point where rupture becomes inevitable: only, before it is reached, we know how to go into reverse. If we don't, the happy married life goes up in smoke! The red light hasn't shown as yet for Pauline or Fontane, but the green has gone out. Keep a careful eye on what happens now!'

3

IN the course of the next few weeks Hervé went several times to the house at Neuilly, on a variety of pretexts: to borrow a book, to ask advice. These visits gave him a great deal of pleasure, which was inspired not by vanity but affection. He had the impression that Fontane was uneasy, perhaps unhappy. Not that he complained to the young man. His utterances remained ironic, but his pleasing, and slightly ceremonious courtesy did little to conceal a weariness which might have had in it something of despair.

Though he grew increasingly fond of Fontane, Marcenat was compelled to admit to feeling some disappointment. While living in his remote countryside, he had looked on the possibility of getting to know Guillaume Fontane as in the nature of a lofty ambition. Then, suddenly, he had found himself being received by his god as a friend, almost as an equal. But now that the longed-for meeting had come about, what did he find? – An ironical, peevish, and slightly frivolous individual who seemed to be more in search of a guide than capable of guiding others. What, precisely, *was* Fontane's outlook? What were his views on life and death? Had he a moral code? political beliefs? religion in any form? One could listen to him for hours without getting any answer to these questions, because he was careful, as soon as he had taken a step in one direction, to take another, away from it. This behaviour was accepted by his readers because, in their eyes, he belonged to that small number of the elect whose reticence is held to be enigmatic, whose escapism is interpreted as subtlety.

Hervé had, for some time now, given up all hope of the invitation to luncheon which, once, Madame Fontane had casually, and vaguely, suggested. Then, all of a sudden, uncertainty was blown to the winds, not by an impersonal card, but by a letter written in Pauline's own hand, in which he was asked to share their midday meal on the following Sunday – 'quite informally, so that we may have an opportunity to talk freely'.

'About what', he thought, 'can this not very free-tongued lady want to talk with such audacious freedom?'

He accepted. The butler with the clerical manner received him with a faintly secretive and discreet smile, which seemed meant to show the visitor that he was now regarded as an old friend of the family. Fontane seemed, as always, pleased to see him. But, what was even more remarkable, Madame Fontane's face appeared to light up when Hervé entered the room. 'This is all very odd,' he thought, 'it is almost as though she has something to ask of me. What in the world can I, a poor weakling, do for this all-powerful hostess?' But he was not wrong, for, as soon as they had sat down to table, in a room to which stained-glass windows gave a crepuscular air, she opened fire.

'We have invited you alone, because an idea has occurred to us in which we think you might be interested. An English publisher has recently written to my husband to say that he is planning a series of short lives of

22

contemporary writers. He wants to include several French men of letters, of whom Guillaume would be one, and is anxious that these biographies should be written by young authors, his intention being to confront two generations – a by no means bad idea. We should like nothing better than for you to undertake the volume on Guillaume, should you find such a project tempting. We know already that you have a very complete knowledge of his work. As to his life, I can supply you with all the necessary information.'

Fontane, who, so far, had taken no part in the conversation, showed signs of embarrassment. He raised his hand.

'Before going any further,' he said to his wife, 'I think we should find out whether such a task appeals to this young man. He has books of his own to write. I see no reason why he should feel obliged to concern himself with my life, and especially not as a commissioned piece of work.'

'Oh! that doesn't bother me!' said Hervé. 'Wasn't one of your finest pieces of writing the result of a commission? But I can't help wondering whether some professional critic, with a high reputation, might not be better qualified for – '

'It is less a question of criticism', broke in Madame Fontane briskly, 'than of portraiture, of personal impressions linked by a biographical sketch.'

Fontane was impatiently drumming on the table with his fingers.

'My dear,' he said: 'no one wants to know how *you* see this book. If he agrees to write it, it will be *his* book, and he must be free to follow out his own ideas. Are you claiming the right to – hm dictate to him – as well?'

Embarrassed by these first signs of a domestic tiff,

Hervé, very unusually for him, took sides with Madame Fontane and tried to change the subject. Nothing was easier than to launch Guillaume on a prolonged monologue by bringing up the names of his favourite authors. Hervé murmured something about Joubert, and the storm withdrew in a soft shower of anecdotes and quotations.

When coffee had been served in the drawing-room, Pauline Fontane said to her husband:

'You haven't forgotten, have you, that you're talking on Ronsard this afternoon to an association of Literary Agents? You haven't much time.'

'Gracious! so I am! And Ronsard, too – it's got to be good. I hope our young friend will forgive me.'

Hervé remained alone with Madame Fontane; which was what she wanted.

'Well?' she said, with an air of determination: 'Are you prepared to undertake this little book?'

'If the publisher – and the model – want me to, yes, madame. Monsieur Fontane's work has had a very special influence on me.'

'That is what your Larivière cousin told me. You will find, when you come to know Guillaume better, that the man is no less interesting than his work. He is entirely devoid of pride – perhaps too much so – but that is not, for the moment, the point at issue. It's settled then, that we shall write this book together?'

Hervé gave a start. 'Oh no!' he thought: 'I am not going to let myself be, as her husband puts it, dictated to.'

He did not, however, make any protest, and reflected that this illusory collaboration might enable him to get a closer view of the Fontane household.

4

FROM then on, he had free access to the house. Pauline Fontane would frequently ring him up in the morning. 'I have some papers here which you might find useful: come round at six.' At such times he would find her surrounded by letters and manuscripts, on the subject of which she would keep up a running commentary which was astonishing by reason of its subtlety of analysis. She had taken to pieces the whole of her husband's intellectual and emotional mechanism. This in no way diminished her admiration: she served him faithfully, and, also, her own purposes.

It was not long before Hervé realized precisely what it was that she expected of him. Before his marriage, Fontane had had a long-lasting liaison with a young woman whom he had met when he was teaching at Rennes. The photographs showed her as a fresh and appealing creature. Pauline described her as having been, intellectually, well below the average. This unfortunate Minnie had tried to kill herself when her lover married. Saved by a surgeon with more skill than compassion, she had become resigned.

'What has happened to her?' Hervé asked.

'She died two years ago. She had gone back to her family in Brittany.'

What Madame Fontane wanted was that Marcenat should take up a position against those critics who divided her husband's work into two periods and maintained that the books which belonged to the time when Minnie was in the ascendant were more original than those which came later. When next he found himself alone with the master, Hervé broached the subject.

'Ah! my friend,' said Fontane in melancholy accents, 'if you want to paint a picture of the days when I was starting on my career, you must use a bright, gay palette. At that time I was little, if at all, concerned with the universality of human malice, the vanity of life, the uselessness of everything. I had confidence, first and foremost in myself. I knew that all I wanted was to trim and shape my adjectives, and to bring happiness to a young woman's eyes. But today – art? Yes, to be sure, it still provides me with a certain amount of amusement. Only, nowadays, everyone, myself included, knows my limitations as a colourist. The veriest parodist is familiar with my recipes of antithetical adjectives. You could do the Fontane stuff, if you wanted to. Friendship? – well, the alternations of failure and success have shown me, only too clearly, the inconstancy of those in whom I most believed.'

That was one of his Jeremiad days.

'You are ungrateful, *cher maître*. I can think of no one with so little right to complain. Your wife lives only for you: your work stands a good chance of survival: some of the most outstanding men of the day are among your friends. What more do you want?'

'I want nothing. It is just that I find life full of vanity and bitterness. Still – I have probably got ten, fifteen years to look forward to – and how, I ask you, do I spend the irreplaceable minutes? Writing books I don't believe in, seeing a lot of foreigners who don't understand me, when all I long for is to be allowed to enjoy the last rays of the sun in peace, reading again a few poets, a few wise men, and finding once more, in the company of the young, something of the savour of life.'

'It is I, now, who do not understand,' said Hervé. 'If that is what you really want, you can have it with the greatest of ease. You can write only what you want to write, and, as for youth, can you not see, from my example, that it is only too glad to flock round you?'

'No doubt, my friend, no doubt. But I don't go out of my way to find disciples; I have never wished to influence the minds of others. With you, it is different. You are kind enough to listen to my broodings and my groans : but, because you accept me as I am, you don't tear up my roots. Renewal can come to me only through the simple, through those who will talk to me about everything under the sun – except myself. Ingenuousness, an almost animal ingenuousness, is what I thirst for, yet it is of that I am deprived.'

On this particular evening, Marcenat found him so despondent that he could not keep himself, next day, from describing to Madame Fontane her husband's state of melancholy, and suggesting that what he needed was a change in his way of life.

'Don't worry,' she said, with a faint shrug. 'He is always like this between books. Guillaume is, in some ways, a manic-depressive. He has his periods of creativeness which coincide with his moments of well-being. As soon as a book is finished, he enters on a process of gestation which, at first, is painful. Time and time again I have heard him say that he is getting old, that he is sick of writing, that he has nothing more to say, or that the subject he has chosen will yield him nothing. I listen, and I wait. Sooner or later a day always comes when his work begins to go better, when his temper improves, when his pessimism gives way to a mood of happy excitement – and then, the crisis is over.'

The authority with which she said all this was like that of a skilled psychiatrist speaking of a patient.

'You know him better than I do, madame : but don't you think that a change of environment would be good for him, and a chance of meeting more young people?'

'I know what you mean,' she said bitterly. 'That Larivière cousin of yours has been telling you that I keep Guillaume shut away, that I suffer from an almost pathological jealousy, that I prevent him from meeting young women, that I am harming his work!'

'Edmée has said nothing of the sort!'

'If she hasn't, then her sister has, or one of her women friends. I know what is being said about us, but you will see, when you have spent more time in our company, how untrue it is. I admit that I used to be jealous in the early years of our marriage. Today, Guillaume is no longer a young man, and we have been married for twenty-five years. I leave him perfectly free to stray, and if he doesn't, that is because he has no wish to. Sometimes, when he has a "rave" letter from a girl student, he goes into a daydream, but that lasts only for a short while, and he returns to his desk, where he finds his real happiness, and to me, because I am one of the implements which make his work possible, on a level with his fountain-pen or his Littré.'

In the course of the long conversation which followed, Hervé decided that she was a wise and easy-going woman, and that, all things considered, the master was in good hands.

5

ABOUT this time he was seeing a good deal at the Larivières of a young artist, Wanda Nedjanine, who did pencil portraits, and was a friend of Edmée's two sons. She dressed with an almost affected simplicity. Edmée, a severe critic in matters of art, spoke with respect of Wanda's drawings, and gave proof of her sincerity by hanging one of them between her Chagall and her Dufy.

'Seriously, Hervé, don't you think that girl has something very near genius?'

'Genius is a dangerous word,' he replied: 'but she certainly has style. What's her background?'

'Wanda's background? I don't know much more than you about that. Her family was White – or Pink – Russian, and came to Paris at the time of the Revolution. Wanda was brought up to speak both Russian and French, which accounts for her slight accent – the way she rolls her r's. Now that she is working, she no longer lives with her parents, but has a studio at the far end of a courtyard in the rue de Rennes. I've been to see her there. Her beauty brings her a lot of orders. François' boss, Larraque, has sat to her, and he, God knows, is not overburdened with patience! I have an idea that her admirers don't get much for their pains. In politics, in spite of her origins, she is, I gather from what the boys tell me, very much Left-wing. Actually, I think her attitude of revolt is more a matter of sentiment than of ideology, but I'm pretty certain that she hates the lot of us.'

A few days later, Hervé had this diagnosis confirmed. He happened to be present during a discussion between Edmée and some of her women friends about the difficulties of life in the modern world. Noting that Wanda was silent, he sat down beside her, and said:

'Have you no contribution to make?'

'Why should I? I don't want to be rude, but how dare a woman like Edmée Larivière talk about "difficulties"? She knows she has only to write a cheque to be fed, dressed, and adorned. When she wants to go anywhere, she has only to get into the long white car which is always standing at her front-door, or to press the button of a lift. Her life is a succession of miracles. To have any real understanding of what day-to-day life entails she ought to have to wait for a bus in the rain, climb six flights of stairs on foot, and count over, again and again, the few francs she has left on the twenty-fifth of every month.'

All this she poured out in a low voice. Her eyes were bright with anger.

'True,' said Hervé; 'all the same, *you* don't seem to have done so badly where material goods are concerned.'

'For the last twelve months,' she admitted, 'things have been going better. But before that I had two terrible years – bad enough to drive one to suicide. Just now I seem to be riding pretty on the snob tide. I'd better get what I can while the going's good – it won't last.'

Hervé looked at her. She had exquisitely formed features, the purity of which was shown off to advantage by very black hair drawn tightly over her ears. Suddenly, an idea came to him. The English publisher had asked for a portrait of Fontane to use as frontispiece to the small book on which he was engaged. Why should not Wanda do it?

'Guillaume Fontane?' she said: 'I know who he is right enough, but I've never read a word he's written. D'you think he's any good? I've got the impression that he's a terrible stick-in-the-mud.'

'You laugh at snobbery,' he said, 'but you're as much of a snob as anybody else. Fontane is no longer as modish as he once was among the advanced cliques. He has had so much more than his fair share of adoration, that the only thing left for people to do now is to abuse him. But I *know*, and you would know too, if you looked at his books, that he is part of the great French tradition – like Chateaubriand or Flaubert. . . .'

'I'm not a Frenchwoman, and I don't like either Chateaubriand or Flaubert.'

'Whom do you like?'

'The writers of my own country: Pushkin, Gogol, Dostoevsky, Chekhov . . . as to yours, well, I'm pretty keen on Proust.'

'A good choice, but Proust, you know, was a great admirer of Chateaubriand – and of Flaubert.'

She shook her head.

'Maybe. On second thoughts, I'm not all that sure about Proust. After all, he thought that life only really begins in the Boulevard Malesherbes. But my tastes don't matter. One doesn't have to admire a man to paint his portrait. I shall be delighted, if you can arrange it, Hervé.'

'I see only one difficulty : you are a bit too good-looking. Madame Fontane will be uneasy – Look here, she's "at home" on Sundays : what do you say to my taking you along?'

A new face caused as much surprise in the closed circle at Neuilly, as the appearance of a strange dog would have done in the streets of Combray. Wanda's advent set going a wave of curiosity. Alexis regarded with silent disapproval the black sweater which revealed, as much as it concealed, a pair of proudly jutting breasts. But Pauline Fontane received the young woman most affably. The English biography was of great moment to her, and Edmée had prepared the ground by showing her some of Wanda's sketches.

'They seem to me quite admirable,' Pauline had said; 'her line is true and scrupulous. She is not likely, I should say, to distort Guillaume's face, as most of these young artists do, in order to assert *themselves*. I think it's a *very* good idea.'

It was agreed, in the course of that first visit, that Wanda should do the portrait in Fontane's study at Neuilly, so as to interrupt his work as little as possible. A fortnight later, meeting Hervé at Edmée Larivière's, she expressed her thanks.

'It really is a piece of cake for me. He's a perfect lamb, and says the most charming things. He's a good sitter.

He's got the sort of shyness which I find amusing. Besides, you can have no idea of the prestige he enjoys, even among *my* friends.'

'I can, quite easily : I told you how it would be.'

'I know. But, you see, I didn't altogether trust your taste, Hervé dear. But Bob and Bobby, who are nothing if not up to the minute, are loud in their enthusiasm. "You've landed a big fish, Wanda," they said when they heard. "Be careful not to let him get away." '

'Is he trying to get away?' asked Hervé : 'I should be very much surprised if he were.'

'To be perfectly honest, so should I !'

She laughed, and there was a note of cruelty in the sound. He noticed that she had a rather thick neck, strangely out of keeping with the delicate modelling of her face.

6

ONE Monday morning, Pauline Fontane rang Hervé up. There was nothing unusual in that : what was surprising was the note in her voice. For all her strong-mindedness she sounded agitated and uneasy.

'We didn't see you yesterday,' she said. 'Guillaume's far from well. He's running a temperature, and the doctor, who's just left, has mentioned the possibility of pleurisy. He was coughing a good deal on Friday, and yesterday evening he insisted on going out in this frightful weather to dine with some foreign publisher or other, in Montparnasse. He didn't take the car, because of its being Sunday, or so he said, and had to walk a long way in the rain, because he couldn't find a taxi. When he got home, he was in a bad way. So now, here he is, in bed for the next week, and all through his own fault.'

'Are you sure, madame, that it's not serious?'

'Oh! quite. Dr Gaulin gave me his word. He says there was no reason why you shouldn't come round and see the patient – that is why I rang you. Guillaume's very anxious to see you at once, though it would have been more sensible to wait for a day or two. Still, you know what he's like when his mind is made up.'

'I'll be along about noon, madame. That will suit me admirably.'

He found her in the library. She had opened the post, and was engaged in answering the more urgent letters in her bold, masculine handwriting.

'I am so glad to see you,' she said. 'He has already asked three times whether you have come yet. He is behaving like a child ... a very bad patient. Come with me.'

She led him up to the first floor, which he had never yet seen. As they crossed the landing, he took a look at the famous Watteaus of the Boersch collection.

'We'll go through my room,' she said.

The brocade curtains on either side of the huge Regency bed were held up by chubby gilded cupids. On the walls were an impudent pink Boucher, and a portrait of Fontane. The bathroom had a mosaic floor and was panelled in a diamond pattern. It gleamed with cut-glass bottles heavily stoppered with silver. The bath was concealed under a loose-cover, which, thought Hervé, had a very ridiculous effect. Madame Fontane knocked at a door, and opened it.

'Here he is!' she said to her husband.

Fontane was wearing white pyjamas. The pillows had disarranged his hair, and he was unshaven.

'Welcome, my friend,' he said, and began to cough. 'How good of you to have taken all this trouble. Sit down by the bed. Pauline, give him a chair, and then leave us.'

33

She brought the chair, and leaned on the foot of the bed:

'What would you like for your lunch, Guillaume?' she asked. 'Gaulin said that – '

He wriggled impatiently:

'We will discuss that later! I should be very much obliged, just now, if you would leave us.'

He was silenced by a distressing fit of coughing. Pauline Fontane, deeply hurt, did not insist.

'I can see that I am in the way,' she said.

She went out through the bathroom, leaving the door ajar. Hervé had the impression that she was still in the adjoining room. He was about to get up to close the door, which was screened by a curtain, but changed his mind, thinking that if Madame Fontane really was there, she might think it a discourteous and somewhat suspect action on his part. Guillaume Fontane, who had not noticed his momentary embarrassment, beckoned to him to come nearer. He seemed to be in the grip of fever, or of some lively emotion. His face was far redder than it should have been.

'Nearer still, my friend,' he said in a whisper, 'nearer. . . . I want you to do me a favour. I had arranged to meet Wanda this afternoon. She is an interesting and intelligent young woman, and I make a point of seeing her now and again. I was to have gone to tea with her at the studio. Naturally, that is now out of the question, but how am I to let her know?'

'What is the difficulty?' said Hervé. 'Doesn't Madame Fontane know about this engagement?'

'She knows nothing, nothing at all, any more than she knows that it was with Wanda that I was dining yesterday. But don't go getting ideas. If Pauline were a different sort of woman I would have told her. It is really a very innocent situation – but you don't know her as I do.'

34

It was clear to Marcenat that Fontane, under the influence of his fever, might say more than he intended. He did his best, therefore, to put an end to a conversation which, for all he knew, Pauline could overhear.

'Don't worry, *cher maître*. I will ring her up as soon as I have left you.'

'Thank you – thank you. But that is not all. Tomorrow is her birthday, and I've bought her a small Picasso drawing. I was to have picked it up today at the Ezec Galleries, you know the place I mean, in the rue de Seine, behind the Institute. Could you possibly manage to look in there yourself, and see that Wanda gets it? Give me my chequebook – it is in the top drawer of the chest-of-drawers, and my fountain-pen, which you will find on the table.'

Hervé got to his feet. Through the half-open door he caught a glimpse of a black dress. He had been right about Madame Fontane: she was still there. When he returned to the bed, he laid a finger on his lips. He intended the gesture as a warning, but Fontane did not grasp its significance.

'I'll make the cheque out to you,' he said, 'just to avoid awkward questions. All you'll have to do is endorse it. I know you won't mind going to see the charming Wanda. Ah! my friend, you can have no idea what it means to me to find at my age a – hm – genuine pleasure. Only to look at that young woman, to watch her live, to listen to her ... Last week' – a fit of coughing interrupted him – 'I wrote a poem about her – the first time for years that I've done such a thing: a sort of *Élégie de Marienbad*. I'll read it to you when I'm well again, though I shan't, of course, publish it. "*This book is for the good, not for the wicked.*" Ah! Goethe! there was a lucky man. I must re-read his correspondence with Bettina. He was seventy, she, nineteen. For him, it was an extraordinary spiritual

35

renewal. But he was Goethe, and a free man: whereas I am a slave!'

'How you do exaggerate, *cher maître*!'

'No, my friend, no. You can have no conception what Madame Fontane is like! Don't think that I fail to recognize her very great virtues. She has given me everything: she lives only for me, and it is but natural that she should demand much in return. She laid a charm on one whole period of my life. My trouble is that her beneficent powers are now exhausted. Never forget, my friend, that a married man can no longer develop according to the laws of his own being. He has lost the right to change, and, consequently, to live, unless he can carry with him into that change the other half of himself – who clings to her own ideas. . . .'

He coughed, spat, panted.

'Don't talk so much,' said Hervé, 'you'll only make yourself worse: besides –'

'Wait. Just one word more – what I am going to say will be useful to you. Think of the period we live in. The world is moving into a time of complete upheaval. The class to which Pauline and I belong is destined to disappear as completely as did the nobility of 1788. I mean precisely that. I'm not saying it's a good or a bad thing, but merely looking facts in the face. If one is to remain young one has to feel with those who are young today. To accept the present is not to deny the past, but to create what, tomorrow, will be the past of a new world. That is the strict truth. Who, less than I, clings to honours, wealth, an acquired position? What do I ask for? A whitewashed cell with a mattress on the floor, fresh water, and fruit. I am ready, my friend, to become an ascetic or a prophet, but I am bound hand and foot to the skeleton of a dead society, bound by my wife's pearls, by the ribbons, red or blue, in which she has seen fit to strangle me. I have never had any ambition ! – but she, ah ! she . . . a woman at once intelligent, shrewd, loyal, proud, and pig-headed . . . she has made use of me to help her to the top – the top of what? Whom does she find there? Those who frequent Sundays. She thinks them brilliant because they are for the most part men who have "arrived". That they may have done, but, as someone has said, in what state? The high peaks ! – deserted, frozen, covered deep in the eternal snows ! If I can't tear myself free, I am lost for ever.'

'If that is how you feel, *cher maître*, seek a change of scene. If necessary, go away, as Tolstoy did : that would have a certain grandeur about it.'

'Impossible, my friend. What excuse could I offer? Pauline is perfect, and beyond reproach.'

'Madame Fontane certainly does not deserve anything of the kind,' said Hervé, not without some show of impatience, 'but still less does she deserve to have her life poisoned by your ill-humour.'

The young man got up and, once again, glanced uneasily towards the door.

'Must you really go?' said Fontane. 'Well, if you must, you must. Remember what I have asked of you – the telephone message, the Ezec Galleries – good-bye, my friend, for the time being, and come again soon.'

On the landing, Hervé found Madame Fontane.

The look she gave him was unwavering, imperious, tragic.

'I should like a word with you before you go,' she said.

7

SHE led him down the stairs without a word, and into a room on the ground floor, smaller than Fontane's study, which she had grown accustomed to think of as her own. The walls were covered with photographs depicting the Fontane pair in many different settings: before the Pyramids; in Toledo; in Florence; in Oxford, with Fontane in a doctor's robes; in the cemetery of Eyoub; at Weimar. The oldest in date had turned yellow, but it was possible to make out Pauline looking young and slim, with a delicate face under an old-fashioned *coiffure*. On the later prints, which were sharper in outline, she had thickened, and Fontane who, at thirty, had looked slightly absurd in jackets too short for him, had acquired with the passage of the years the same appearance as he had now, and was shown wearing well-cut clothes.

Several times already, when Madame Fontane had admitted him to this sanctuary, Hervé Marcenat had savoured, with something of melancholy, the touching synthesis of these two lives. But today he had eyes only for the drawn and pallid face of the woman before him. She dropped into an odd-looking Gothic armchair.

'I heard everything,' she said.

'I knew that, madame – and, if you will allow me to say, with the utmost respect – '

'No, no, please! I, too, knew that you knew, and judged the extent of your fears by the cautious nature of your replies. You may not believe it, but when I left you alone with Guillaume, I had not the least intention of eavesdropping. I had paused in the bathroom to arrange certain medicines which had just been delivered from the chemist's ... but when the first words of that incredible confession reached me, I lost my head. I thought that I should be bound to make a noise if I opened my bedroom door, that Guillaume would detect my presence, that he would be angry. In short, I dared not move. Can anyone ever know for certain why or how one behaves at such moments? The fact remains that I heard everything, and you can imagine what a shock it was for me.'

She was trembling. Her high-bridged nose had suddenly taken on the colour of wax. Hervé, though he pitied her profoundly, felt that, in this conflict, his sense of loyalty compelled him to take the master's side.

'This is a most deplorable situation, madame: but the fault –'

Pauline clung to the young man's arm with the desperation of a dying woman.

'It is my sense of responsibility that is at issue! I am fighting for him, not for myself!' she exclaimed. 'Whether he does or does not run after a woman who is young enough to be his daughter, matters nothing to me. Had he told me about this business, do you really think that I should have set my face against it? I have been jealous in the past, wildly jealous, but I am so no longer!'

'If that is so, madame, I fail to understand your emotion. Since you were prepared to tolerate –'

'I was prepared to tolerate the sensuality of an ageing man, but not his repudiation of our marriage! What really appalled me was the picture he drew, the picture of an ambitious woman who was ready to make use of him in her struggle to reach certain unspecified "heights"! He appears to have forgotten everything! When I first knew Guillaume, he was an obscure professor who wrote in his spare time, and wrote very well, though there was no public for his books. Can you really believe that I should have attached myself to a man like that if I had been ambitious? Ambitious of what? I had all I wanted. I was young and free. I entertained in my house the most brilliant society to be found in the worlds of politics and letters. What need had I of a little second-rate professor who had produced an unsaleable volume of essays? But I was in love with him, and, far from *clinging*, put all I had of power and prestige at his disposal. I became his mistress long before I knew for certain he would marry me, and that, for a woman brought up as I had been, was the greatest proof I could give of love, as is the fact that I am now baring my heart to you. And he loved me. He may find that difficult to remember, but I can show you the letters he wrote to me at the time.'

With trembling hands she bent over one of the drawers of the table. The movement loosened the heavy coils of her hair which suddenly collapsed in a shower of tortoise-shell combs. No one could have recognized in this distraught and haggard woman the proud and arrogant Madame Fontane.

'My keys,' she muttered, 'where are my keys? I can't see a thing!'

'They are in the left-hand drawer, madame, but it is really quite unnecessary – '

'Unnecessary! No ... no. ... You have heard the prosecution, now you must listen to the defence!'

From a cardboard box she took a bundle of letters tied with ribbon. Hervé recognized Fontane's graceful, sloping, and deliberately archaic handwriting. Pauline was struggling with the ribbon.

'I can't undo it. Take them, monsieur, and read!'

Hervé, feeling distinctly ill at ease, hastily glanced through a few of the letters. He read with a feeling of intense emotion. Here were the effusions, banal, yet sublime as love itself, of a man who had just found a mistress capable of inspiring him.

Pauline Fontane was looking at him with an expression in which curiosity was mingled with supplication. He felt ashamed to be reading such intimate letters before her very eyes, and handed the packet back to her. She seemed calmer now, and had stopped trembling. She got up, looked at herself in the glass, and said:

'Oh, what a sight I am! ... my hair! ... I really must apologize.'

She gathered the strands together, twisted them, and replaced the combs.

'Perhaps when Guillaume is more himself,' she said, 'he will recognize the past for what it was. Just now, he is busy making a case against me, pretending that I have kept him from understanding the times in which we are living! That grievance is purely imaginary, as he very well knows – a virtuous excuse which he has fabricated because he wants to rationalize his desire for a younger woman. I, a conservative! I, a reactionary! – what nonsense! Politics bore me. If I really thought that Guillaume would be happier leading a modest life in retirement, I should be only too willing to go away with him to some place far from Paris. But he wants nothing of the sort. He has told you that he would be contented with a *white-washed cell*! That is one of his favourite themes, but it has no basis in fact. He has to have his books around him, and a house chock-full of bookshelves doesn't keep itself clean. When people come to see him in the evening, he likes to keep them to dinner. But it is impossible to improvise a meal. Men know as little about the mysteries of the kitchen as the passengers of a liner know about coal-bunkers. I am the captain, and I am responsible. Let us not beat about the bush: is not all this craving for austerity, this scorn of success, this purely verbal humility, in his case, just a lie?'

'That I do not know, madame: but if it is, then it is a wholly unconscious lie. He really thinks he is speaking the truth.'

She was now perfectly calm. The Gorgon with disordered locks had given place to Madame Fontane.

'The truth? I am not so sure. He complains of my Sundays, but he loves to see his friends at them, and to show

41

off. Besides, what else does this young woman do, in Montparnasse, than make him the centre of much the same sort of gathering? Oh yes, I know from Dominique, Edmée's son, that only last week the wild creature gave a Fontane cocktail-party in her studio! If her friends drink gin instead of tea, read Lautréamont instead of Baudelaire, it is just a question of different generations. That fashion, too, will become outmoded.'

At that moment, the prolonged, impatient ringing of a bell reached their ears.

'That is Guillaume,' she said with a sigh. 'I'd better go and see what he wants. You had better carry out your various commissions. But make sure that he really has signed the cheque. He so often forgets to: and that leads to all sorts of complications.'

8

OLD Madame Ezec smiled when Marcenat gave her the cheque.

'Ah! that Monsieur Fontane!' she said: 'somebody's pulling the wool over his eyes!'

Drawing in hand, Hervé made his way to the rue de Rennes. Wanda opened the door to him. She was wearing grey slacks and a red sweater, which set off her pretty face to advantage and gave her the look of an hermaphrodite Shelley.

'It's only me, Wanda. As I told you over the telephone, our friend's in bed. He hopes you will accept this small drawing as a birthday present.'

'I bet it's the Picasso from old Mother Ezec's. It really is too good of him. But come in, won't you? Hang your coat over the stair-rail or chuck it on the floor. Yes, it *is* the Picasso! – what an old lamb Guillaume is! I'm terribly sorry he's not well – unless, of course, the whole story has been invented by his wife!'

'It's genuine enough, I swear, Wanda. I saw him with my own eyes shaking with fever and coughing his guts up. He's mad at not being able to keep his date with you. But, now that you *have* introduced Madame Fontane into the conversation, I think I ought, perhaps, to tell you something about the situation.'

'What situation?'

'The one you've created by coming between the two halves of this domesticated couple. My dear Wanda, whether intentionally or not, you've loosed off a drama! This very morning Pauline Fontane broke down completely in my presence, and sobbed her heart out because she overheard something her husband was saying to me in the next room.'

'What was he saying? You're being very odd today, Hervé, quite incoherent and mysterious. Come on, out with it, and no beating about the bush. I want to know *exactly* what Guillaume said.'

'He was moaning about their married life, complaining that he knew nothing about the modern world, praising you to the skies – in fact, talking in a way that must have been extremely painful for his wife to hear.'

'Serves her right, for listening at key-holes.'

'No, seriously, I felt most awfully sorry for her.'

Wanda lit a cigarette with great deliberation.

'Well, what exactly are you getting at?'

'It's I who ought to be asking *you* that. What are you hoping for from this conquest? I can't believe that a young and lively woman like yourself seriously suggests that Guillaume Fontane, who's close on sixty, should divorce his wife and marry you?'

'You know my views on marriage perfectly well.

No one could well be more independent than I am.'

'You're not, by any chance, planning to take him as your lover?'

'My dear Hervé, would it surprise you very much to hear that I am planning *nothing at all*? You ask me what I am expecting to get out of this conquest. I simply don't know. To start with, I had no idea that it was a conquest. I knew, of course, that Fontane finds me attractive, and likes seeing me. But it never occurred to me that his wife might find any cause for alarm in so little. But if the shaft has really gone home, as you say it has, then I'm to be congratulated!'

'But, Wanda, you can't possibly be in love with him?'

'Love is such a very vague word: there's something of everything in it – bestial violence, tender affection, mortal sickness. ... And why couldn't I "possibly" be in love with Guillaume? You don't know him. When he's alone with me, he's perfectly adorable. He laughs, he says the most charming things. We lunch together out in the country, and dine in Paris at bistros. Poor Guillaume! He's always trying to find excuses – such artless, transparent excuses – for getting closer to me, for taking my arm, my waist. He's terribly sweet. And then, there's something of the child in him, too, you know. It's really rather touching, the way he lies down on the divan, and asks me to "amuse him". No matter how little I give, and I do give awfully little, he's so touchingly grateful. I think I've a good deal of influence with him, and that's important. When things started, I told him that I detested the ideas of his world. He replied that it wasn't *his* world. Having discovered that I've got a passion for politics, he tried to get at me through that ... and, to some extent, succeeded. Quite seriously, Hervé, don't you realize what a staggering effect it might have if, on the eve of the

44

elections, Fontane suddenly became vocal about problems which, till now, he has completely ignored? Why, it would be sen-*sa*-tional! That's what I'm going to try to get him to do, and if his wife gets in my way, so much the worse for her!'

'You mean you'd go so far as to make off with her husband?'

'Most certainly, if I could!'

'Then you'd be guilty of a crime – you might as well shoot her and have done with it!'

'A crime? But is there anything more sinister in the world than an old married couple? Philemon and Baucis have always made me feel slightly sick! From the moment when what poor Guillaume calls "authentic" desire has ceased between them, husband and wife ought to separate. There's a couple in this house whom I meet every morning. For the last forty years, so the concierge tells me, they've taken their morning walk together. It's perfectly nauseating, Hervé, to see those two doddering, withered old creatures dragging about side by side and never exchanging a word!'

'Would it be any better if each of them was alone? Besides, the Fontanes are neither doddering nor withered – far from it. You lack humanity, Wanda.'

'On the contrary! It's I who am human, you who are conventional. I'm a Russian, my dear, with a congenital craving for frankness. You French are all suppressed. You keep your feelings and your desires even from yourselves. Yes, you do! You go on, till your last gasp, "laying aside" for your old age! Then, one evening, when the end comes, you discover that you have been dupes, that you've never really lived, and that it's too late: you're finished. It's from that sort of thing that I want to save Guillaume.'

'By killing his wife?'

She leaned forward and looked him in the eyes with an air of amused defiance.

'I'm hard, Hervé dear. Don't think for a moment that I shouldn't be perfectly ready to harm somebody who didn't matter to me, if, by so doing, I could achieve something more important. What's going on in your mind?'

'I was thinking that you must have known a great deal of suffering in the course of your life. Hardness is almost always a form of revenge – or so it seems to me.'

She laughed.

'Hervé Marcenat, or the Confessor! Yes, my dear, I have suffered a great deal. I swear to you that I have had to avoid, like the plague, any temptation to indulge in sensibility and cowardice.'

'And now?'

'Now? – how impatient our Hervé is! He wants to know the end of a story which has scarcely begun. You'll see – *we'll* see. I know no more than you do, what's going to happen. Meanwhile, what about a cup of tea? I'd bought a cake for Guillaume. In the Master's absence, I'd better feed the disciple. I shall charge it all to general overheads!'

While she was busy boiling the kettle in her tiny kitchen, Hervé, who could never keep away from other people's books, took a good look at Wanda's. She had all the great Russians, translations of Hemingway and Faulkner, Goethe in German, Rimbaud, Lautréamont, Malraux, Sartre – and, at the end of the row, brand-new copies of five of Fontane's books. He opened them. Only a few pages had been cut. She came back into the studio.

They drank their tea.

9

THE illustrated papers published Wanda's portrait of Fontane. He allowed himself to be photographed with it. Some found the confrontation amusing, others, ridiculous. Madame Fontane, who, it was said, was far from well, had given up being seen about with her husband, and no longer answered the telephone. Hervé Marcenat, having been without news of husband and wife for three weeks, went to the rue de la Ferme, where Alexis welcomed him with melancholy unction.

'You will find the house sadly changed, sir: Madame is extremely unwell.'

The young man announced to Fontane that he had nearly finished the small book which he was writing for the English publisher.

'Ah! My friend, what does it matter? *That* is no longer uppermost in my mind. I am deeply concerned about Pauline. Even Gaulin does not know what is the matter with her. You will tell me that doctors never do know, that no one ever knows, anything about sickness. All the same, the members of the medical fraternity can, at least, classify our ailments in carefully labelled compartments, and that, in itself, is reassuring. To be able to call a demon by its name is – hm – half-way to getting rid of him. But I gather that it is impossible to identify the trouble from which my wife is suffering.'

'That seems very curious. What are the symptoms?'

'How shall I describe them? Each morning she gets up and tries to dress. Then she gets a dizzy fit, and lies down again on her bed, where she stays for the rest of the day. As soon as she tries to eat, she feels sick. I have had the lightest possible meals sent up to her, the sort of meals she used to like, but she can keep nothing down, and is getting thinner all the time. It's all very odd and deplorable.'

'What about your work?'

'Don't talk of it! I am a feeble-minded creature. Deprived of the will that spurs me into action, I can do nothing. I spend all day mooning over my favourite authors. In the evenings, in an attempt to shake off my melancholy, I have taken to haunting the restaurants and the theatres. Our young friend, Wanda, has taken pity on my loneliness, and is so good as to give me her company.'

'Does Madame Fontane know that?'

'Not from me, I can assure you! I never mention Wanda to her, and can only hope that others are not so cruel as to do so. She sees nobody.'

When Hervé reported this conversation to Edmée Larivière, she was loud in her blame of both women.

'I am sorry for Pauline,' she said in her blunt way, 'but she is only reaping what she has sown. She has tried to keep her husband on a leash, with the result that he feels a strong need to break loose. With just a little tolerance and humour she could have saved the essentials. Because she wanted to keep everything, she is now running the risk of losing everything. She knows that, and is playing illness as her trump card, so as to get from pity what she can no longer have from affection.'

'But really, Edmée, I can assure you that she is not playing a game. She is being attended by Gaulin who is neither a charlatan nor a fool. He says that he is very worried – thinks she is dangerously ill.'

'That I am quite willing to believe. *Mme Dino has decided to be well and to recover*, said Talleyrand. Madame Fontane has decided to be ill and to take to her bed. When women want to be what Gaulin calls "genuinely" ill, they can be. They are even capable of dying from sheer pride.'

'Why not say, *from love*?'

'The two things are not contradictory. As to the other, the Wanda girl, she's as hard as nails. She thinks that Fontane can be of use to her. She would rather have had a younger man, but chance sent her Fontane. Fair enough! Fontane is *her* trump card, and nothing will make her change her mind. So, we can do nothing. Now I've got that off my chest, let me say that I'm very glad you have talked to me about the situation, because I want to ask your advice on a rather ticklish matter. Bertier, that journalist you met here at luncheon, is very anxious to meet Fontane. I should like to do what I can for him, because he always gives us good write-ups in his papers. Now, the position is as follows. Since Pauline has given up going out, Guillaume, who is completely under the thumb of his young charmer, won't accept invitations unless she is asked too. That, I consider, is in the worst of taste, but I know it to be a fact. I have tried to get him without her, but he has always trotted out some perfectly nonsensical excuse, though, God knows, he is fond of me! All his women friends, Hélène de Thianges, Claire Ménétrier, Isabelle Schmitt, have found themselves up against the same blank wall. On the other hand, Denise Holmann, who has thrown in her hand and passed under the Caudine Forks of the rue de Rennes, has entertained the amazing couple three times in one month! I thoroughly disapprove, but what can one do? Guillaume is like that. I should be only too glad to have the girl: she's got talent and an assured future – but there's Pauline to be considered. If she heard I'd had them here together, she'd never forgive me, and, in my heart of hearts, I shouldn't blame her. I should think myself lacking in loyalty if I

49

asked her husband with somebody else. Tell me what you think I ought to do?'

'I agree with you that it wouldn't be conduct befitting a friend of Pauline's. All the same, I have a feeling that's exactly what you will do.'

'Good for you!' she said, with a laugh. 'Would you care to lunch here on Tuesday, with Fontane, Wanda, and Bertier?'

'So, you've already decided! Why, then, did you ask my advice?'

'Because, if your reaction had been really violent, I should have held my hand. But it is at the best lukewarm – though you don't, perhaps, realize that?'

'Look here, Edmée, what do you want me to say? You are all giving in, and, admittedly, the situation is exceedingly delicate. If I knew *only* Madame Fontane, I should most certainly refuse to meet the other. But Wanda, too, is a friend of mine. How can I take sides?'

'My dear Hervé, when one wants to justify a bad action, one can always find good arguments. Personally, I think it more honest to look our cowardice in the face – which is what I am doing.'

Hervé bridled.

'It isn't a question of cowardice. After all, Guillaume Fontane counts for more with me than his wife.'

She laughed.

'Oh, you men!' she said: 'you're never realistic!'

During the meal, Wanda said little, but when she did open her mouth, she was careful to stress her right to Fontane by her peremptory use of the word 'we'.

'*We* dined at the Place du Tertre. *We* are going to see the Komaroff collection tomorrow.'

Hervé asked when her portrait show at the Ezec Galleries was going to open.

'Private View on 8 June,' she said proudly, 'and Guillaume's going to write the Preface for the catalogue.'

'That, I think, is a great mistake,' remarked Edmée dryly.

'Why?' Wanda retorted. 'Claudel's done the same thing, and Valéry, and lots of others.'

'That was quite a different matter,' said Edmée.

'In what way, different?'

'Well, since you insist, I will be frank with you: because everyone knows how much you admire our friend. It will be said that he's done it to please you, and that will do neither you nor him any good.'

Wanda's face went white with anger.

'Do you suppose', she said, more than ever rolling her r's, 'that Claudel and Valéry didn't feel admiration for the artists they were praising?'

Edmée gave a shrug:

'You know perfectly well that we are not using the word *admiration* in the same sense.'

Having said this, she changed the subject. She had no wish to quarrel with a couple whose relationship might turn out to be a lasting one. Guillaume Fontane gave the impression that he was a willing slave, and, on the whole, a happy one, except when he was asked for news of Pauline. Then his face assumed an expression of decent grief. He raised his eyes to heaven, and shook his head.

Wanda and he left, as they had come, together.

10

PAULINE FONTANE was informed about the Larivière luncheon. With Guillaume, and, later, with Edmée, who was summoned to the rue de la Ferme, she had a violent altercation, as a result of which Fontane, for a few days, at least, behaved rather more circumspectly. He continued to visit Wanda in her studio, but gave up accepting invitations for the two of them together. One evening he begged Hervé Marcenat to share his solitary dinner at Neuilly. When it was over, he took the young man into the garden, where, under the stars, he imparted to him a number of melancholy confidences.

'Ah! my friend – I am by nature an epicurean with little taste for tragedy, yet, here I am, landed with a situation worthy of – hm – Corneille. I cannot, without a sense of shame and ingratitude, allow myself to forget Pauline's scrupulous devotion, and an affection which has been demanding only because it has been absolute. Yet not without feelings of despair would I turn my back upon a sentiment which, doubtless, is the last flicker of a heart now little more than a heap of burnt-out ashes. Truly, my friend, I should be able to write on my misfortunes lines no less moving than those of Rodrigue, since, in my case, the obstacle is my wife, and the cause of the offence, my dearest woman friend.'

'How do matters stand? I confess that I am not up-to-date in this matter of your emotional tangle.'

'Alas! the situation is only too simple! Pauline is getting weaker, of that there can be no doubt. She refuses all food. Her thinness is pitiful. She has lost nearly two stone. But what really frightens me is that Gaulin can no longer conceal from me that he fears the worst. She affects a stoicism which does not take me in. A proof that her ailment is of the spirit rather than the body is that when, as last week, I scarcely leave the house, the doctors at once note a slight improvement. Like all of their tribe, they attribute it to one or other of their – hm – incantations. But, if I stay here, then Wanda gets furious, and warns me that if I continue to neglect her, she will grow tired of waiting. But I cannot give her up: no, that is more than I can face. Since she came into my life, I have been a different man. ... Let us sit for a while on this bench, my friend.'

A delicious fragrance was drifting from a nearby mass of honeysuckle.

'Yes,' went on Fontane, 'a different man. I was complaining to you, a while back, that I had lost the power of work. That is no longer true. You will realize that when I read you the long short-story on which, thanks to Wanda, I am engaged. For a long time, as you know, I have been discontented with my writing, but this is something quite new. Why are you groaning?'

'Because I am afraid, *cher maître*, that you have allowed yourself to be led on by Wanda to treat of subjects which are not really yours. Nothing is more dangerous, whether in a novel or a short story, than the working out of explicit ideas.'

'Pure prejudice! Dear boy – was Tolstoy afraid of explicit ideas? Was Joyce? Was Proust? Did they hesitate to vary their fiction with long literary, or even, political discussions? No, this encounter with youthful tenderness will turn out to be immersion in the Fountain of Youth. Only, you see, I am a man in – hm – torment. I do not wish to harm either of the women concerned.'

'I don't think you'll find that easy.'

'Easy? No ... but perhaps not impossible – if you will help me.'

And so it came about that, in the course of their stroll round the flower-beds, Hervé Marcenat agreed to provide a fragile alibi for the long June afternoon which Fontane spent at the Ezec Galleries on the occasion of the Nedjanine Private View. Wanda insisted on his being with her all the time. Edmée Larivière, after a quick tour of inspection, drew Hervé aside under a palm.

53

'You must admit that all this is quite fantastic! Guillaume's putting on all the airs and graces of a host in his own house! – and, then, that Preface! She forced him to drag in a reference to one of the Nedjanine family who was Marshal of the Imperial Household under Catherine the Great! In the first place, it is probably untrue, and, anyhow, she'd better make up her mind whether she is to be treated as Wanda the good pal or Wanda the exiled Grand-Duchess. And oh! – that passage – which she probably dictated – about her extreme simplicity: *"Always plainly dressed in black, without a single jewel."* It's true she makes a point of never wearing any, not even a watch-bracelet, which is why she's always late – but *plainly dressed*, indeed! That's certainly not true since Guillaume came on the scene!'

'Why this passion, Edmée? Why this vehemence? What has she done to you?'

'She has spoiled a friendship which I valued highly.'

All the same, the critics were loud in their praise of the portraits. Bob and Bobby, that curious male pair with whom Wanda was so intimate, were exultant.

'You've done it this time!' said Bob. 'You're well and truly launched. If you didn't happen to have talent, that'd be neither here nor there, but, since you're stuffed full of it – recognition is of prime importance. Your girl friends have been waiting at the corner of the street, to give you a helping hand, if necessary. But you've swept the board unaided, and given them something to boast about, and no mistake!'

Fontane, Hervé, Bob, and Bobby went with Wanda to celebrate the great day at Montmartre. Guillaume was delighted by this little escapade, by Wanda's show of affection, which took the form of her clinging to his arm in the most wifely fashion, and by the little squares planted with chestnuts and filled with open-air cafés.

A few days later, Wanda set off for the south, as the guest of Bob and Bobby, who shared a house at Villefranche.

'If you would like to join us, Guillaume, dear,' she said to Fontane, who was in low spirits, 'they'd be absolutely thr-r-illed. The villa's only a fisherman's shanty, but you would have the best room, there would be lots of pretty girls for you to look at on the beach. It would make me so happy to be living, at last, under the same roof with you. You could be as mad as a hatter, and they'd fix up somewhere for you to work in.'

'I'd much rather you were staying on in Paris,' he said, 'my wife . . .'

'Sorry!' she said dryly, 'but I can't do without my three months of sunshine. I shall expect you.'

But Pauline was in no fit state to leave Neuilly, and Fontane was sufficiently clear-sighted to realize that he could not desert her. Hervé Marcenat dropped back into his old habit – for some time discontinued – of going almost every evening to the rue de la Ferme. Madame Fontane, knowing that Wanda was at a safe distance, ceased to be suspicious, and encouraged her husband to go out with the young man. The Master took a simple-minded pleasure in keeping in contact with the places to which Wanda had introduced him. Everything she liked, pictures, gramophone-records, films, and food, had a surprisingly high degree of prestige in his eyes. The summer became excessively hot, and the young women in the Montparnasse cafés wore flimsy, bright-coloured dresses.

II

AFTER 14 July, the four thousand persons who regard themselves as the leaders of society because they go to bed late, left Paris for the seaside and the country. Fontane, heroic and plaintive, remained faithful to his conjugal duties. His wife's health was improving. She got up for a short while each day, and rested on the sofa, dressed in a very old wrap, the transparent gauze of which revealed a pattern of faded gold on black velvet. She was still deathly pale, but, when she received Marcenat for the first time, he was surprised to find that, like actresses interrupted during a rehearsal, who can slip back readily into the atmosphere of the stage once the disturbance is over, she had taken up again, without any apparent effort, the role of a brilliant and animated hostess.

'Good evening, Hervé,' she said (she had never before called him by his Christian name): 'I often think of you, and always with feelings of gratitude. It is good of you to stay on in Paris because of us, really, very good. . . . No one, better than you, can keep an eye on Guillaume while I am out of action. But it won't be for long. Only this afternoon, Gaulin said that he was very satisfied with me – talks about getting me into the garden next week. Meanwhile, do, please, go out somewhere with Guillaume this evening. It will take his mind off his troubles: the poor fellow is having a pretty dismal summer.'

The night was as heavy as lead, without a breath of air. Marcenat had taken Fontane to a river-barge which had been turned into a restaurant. All round them, people were talking English, German, and Spanish. Fontane was in a complaining mood. He detested this heat, he said, and

56

ever since Wanda had gone away he had been unable to do any work.

'You'd have found it even hotter in the south,' said Hervé.

'Nonsense! In the south there is always a breeze off the sea. Our young friend writes to me that the evenings on the beach are divine. If I were with her, I should think so, too. Read what she says.'

He took a letter from his pocket. Hervé recognized Wanda's strong, virile handwriting. He read:

The sky is blue, the sea is blue, my thoughts are blue. When Bobby brought me my breakfast-tray, he said: 'A letter for you!' I stretched a sleepy hand through the mosquito-net. A little later, I was blushing because of all the nice things you had written. My heart is full of thoughts of you, but they are demanding thoughts, vigorous thoughts. Guillaume dear, why don't you come and join me here? The sea, the noisy, shabby harbour, the dockers stripped to the waist – all these things would make you in love with life, whereas Paris and the people of Paris in town suits and stiff collars only give you the hump. Are you working less well? Have you finished *my* story? I often think about it. My friends pull my leg because I no longer find it possible to open my mouth without saying 'Fontane'. How happy you'd be here when the white sails are hoisted and the motor-boats go careering over a violet-coloured sea with their loads of gay, red-faced sailormen. Come soon, Guillaume. You'll find me frying my back, my front, my legs and my arms on a blazing-hot terrace. Come! – life is beautiful, and you will help me to love it.

Hervé conjured up twin visions of a sick woman in an outmoded dress and a bathing-girl in next to nothing at all.

'Obviously,' he said, handing the letter back to Fontane, 'it is very tempting if –'

They could feel the distant threat of a lowering storm. Fontane complained of a headache.

'This storm that won't break is a good image of my state of mind. Passions rumble and roll, but it is elsewhere, alas! that the longed-for clouds send down the rain for which my poor arid heart is thirsting.'

When the night grew cooler, this mood passed.

'If, in a week's time, Pauline is still on the mend,' he said with a greedy note in his voice, 'I shall ask for a few days leave, and hop down to Villefranche – just there and back, but the time I shall spend there will be – hm – Olympian.'

'You *can't* take that risk!' said Hervé crossly.

For a long time no further word passed between them. Lightning was streaking the sky. Fontane was thinking of a Mediterranean night, of palm-trees swaying in the breeze, of the fragrance of a young body.

'You are hard, my friend,' he said at last, 'very hard.'

'I? – I have never felt fonder of you than at this moment. But you've got to face your responsibilities.'

'I do face them, I most certainly do: but, unfortunately, they are two-sided. My wife is everything to me – if she were to die, I should never cease to look for her consoling presence. But I have been imprudent enough to give Wanda, too – certain hopes.'

'Oh, I feel quite easy in my mind about her,' said Hervé with a shrug.

'And then, there are my own feelings to be considered. You know Wanda as well as I do. You must realize that if I don't go to Villefranche she won't accept defeat. She will break with me, and *that* is something I could not bear! Don't think I'm exaggerating: you know that what I say is true!'

After much discussion, Fontane decided to consult Dr Gaulin. The latter's views were quite definite:

'Madame Fontane would die of grief,' he said; 'I have not the slightest doubt of that. If you ask me how – all I can say is that the human mechanism in such cases is mysterious: action of the emotions on the endocrine glands: intensifying of secretions, with consequent damage to the vital organs. That, roughly speaking, is the pattern. The higher activities control almost everything that happens to the body. Which of the organs would be affected? – the weakest. It varies with different people. I have known numerous cases in which a cancer has been started, beyond all possible doubt, by unhappiness, by worry – the loss of a wife or a husband, disgrace, bankruptcy. In that of Madame Fontane the worst has not yet occurred. She is still hoping against hope. I am convinced that should there be a rupture between you and her, she would lose all hold on life. I must apologize for my seeming brutality, but it is essential that you should know all the elements of the situation.'

As a result of this talk, Guillaume Fontane wrote to Wanda explaining that the state of his wife's health made it impossible for him to go to Villefranche.

12

ILLNESSES which are psychological rather than physical can move with staggering rapidity in the direction of the worse or the better. No sooner was Pauline Fontane convinced that the breach between her husband and Wanda was final, than she began to take nourishment and to put on weight. Colour returned to her face, and her cheeks filled out almost as one looked at them, like a child's balloon when it is being blown up. Dr Gaulin, delighted by this improvement, spoke with some amusement to

Hervé about the seemingly miraculous change in his patient.

'Women are the devil!' he said. 'They think nothing of using death as a means of blackmail, and they win every time!'

Guillaume Fontane seemed badly shaken. For a few days he had enjoyed the feeling of self-satisfaction which abnegation brings. But, with returning strength, Pauline assumed an air of triumph in which there was neither restraint nor tenderness. She seemed not to realize the extent or the nature of the sacrifice made by her husband. Guillaume, she firmly believed, had been the victim of a designing woman, and she, Pauline, had rendered the supreme service of restoring him to reason. She was incapable of imagining that an ardent and painful passion could torment a man with whom she herself had once been furiously in love, though she now regarded him more as a partner, as a machine for the manufacture of books, than as a lover.

For Fontane, rejuvenation through love had, for the past few months, been a high and living hope. The protective attitude now adopted towards him by his wife was deeply hurting. Pauline's behaviour seemed to him as tactless as the manoeuvering of a political party which, having obtained from its adversaries a generous compromise, brings the reconciliation to nothing by treating as a sign of weakness what has been inspired by wisdom and high-mindedness.

'Poor Guillaume!' she said to Hervé, with a superior and indulgent smile. 'At last he has realized that he is close on sixty. Thank heavens he has! That ridiculous infatuation would have brought him nothing but pain.'

'May I be allowed to say to you, madame: go carefully? Monsieur Fontane is still astonishingly young in spirit and in looks. I am pretty sure that women find him just as attractive as ever. He has thrown in his hand out of affection for you, but . . .'

'Not only out of affection, but from necessity! Don't forget how readily that young woman left him.'

'Because she realized that he is deeply attached to you.'

'Poor Guillaume! I really do not know what he would do without me! He knows nothing of life. Have you ever been with him in a railway station or a bank? He's like a moth fluttering round all the pay-counters and booking-offices, singeing its wings!'

Almost every day now she took a short walk, leaning on her husband's arm, and every day the walk grew longer. When, at last, she was able to make the round of the little Lac de Saint-James in the Bois, Fontane proudly related this act of prowess to all his friends. There could be no doubt that he did 'really' love his wife: but her constant use of the words 'poor Guillaume' rasped his nerves. Pity has an unpleasant effect upon its object when it has been aroused, not by a purely external misfortune, but by something deep and personal. Fontane felt diminished, and, in some sense, crippled. His general sense of dissatisfaction was increased and, so to speak, crystallized by the visit of a young journalist, Clement Clementi, who wanted to interview him for a literary magazine.

Clementi was about twenty-two or, at most, twenty-five. He had an angelic expression, but a quick and deliberately aggressive intelligence. From the moment the conversation began, he adopted towards Fontane an arrogant and faintly contemptuous attitude.

'You will remember, sir, that Stendhal said: "I shall have readers in 1880." Do you think that people will be reading your books in 1980?'

'How the devil should I know!' rumbled Fontane. 'It would never have occurred to Voltaire that we should be

61

reading *Candide* today, though he would have been extremely surprised had he been told that no theatre would be playing *Zaïre*. Who could have foreseen what has happened to Baudelaire? Stendhal himself was of the opinion that Racine was finished.'

'That may be true, but it seems pretty certain that only those books can stand up to the passage of the centuries which have contained a pretty large dose of originality. Racine, in his own day, was new. The Romantics of 1830 injected new life into both subject-matter and language. The Surrealists will have their place in the history of our literature. But you, sir, are one of the last exemplars of an admirable, but outmoded tradition.'

Fontane spoke to Hervé of this interview. It was clear that it had made him feel sad and uneasy.

'All the same,' he said, 'the insolence of these young men is beyond all bearing. What I should have said to that second-rate iconoclast is: "You are in a great hurry to bury me alive, yet you, no more than I, can see into the future. It is quite possible that people may still be reading me when you and your gods with feet of clay have been long forgotten. For, don't forget that the verdict of thousands of readers scattered up and down the world is, in some sort, a – hm – prefiguration of posterity." Naturally, I said nothing like that, because I did not want to appear vain. Besides, he wasn't altogether wrong. Ah! my friend, I realize more and more clearly every day what I have lost by living in a confined and monotonous world. Dear Wanda once said to me: "A married man is only half a man." . . . And he's not the best half, either.'

IT was not surprising that, such being Fontane's mood, he should have extended a warm welcome to a visitor from abroad whom Pauline's again effective sieve let through into the master's presence with recommendations from several illustrious persons. This Ovid Petresco, in spite of his Romanian name, was a citizen of the United States. He ran a literary agency in New York, and a lecture bureau, both of them with considerable success. His tactics resembled a torrent in spate. The victim had no chance of standing up to him, because he was never allowed to get a word in edgeways. Arguments of every kind, patriotic, personal, financial, were combined in an assault which lacked neither intelligence nor charm. Ovid Petresco had high hopes that 'the master' would consent to make a lecture tour of South America, ending with visits to New York, Boston, and Philadelphia. He developed the theme with an eloquence which was now lyrical and enthusiastic, now emotional and reproachful when Fontane refused to see where his 'duty' lay.

'Master, you do not know what you are, over there ! In Brazil, in Argentina, in Chile, in Venezuela, Monsieur Fontane he is the Good God – the Good God ! All the ladies they have read your novels; they have them by the heart; you will be received as a Sovereign. And if you do not go, master, what will happen? A lot of midgets, they will make what you call a corner in the bee-utiful French tongue. That is what I, Petresco, will not permit ! At home, over there, I have been educated in the French: I speak the French better than my own language. I wish to be the defender of the French in all the world, and that is why I say to you "Sign!"'

'But, my good friend, I am neither a public speaker, nor a traveller. I know nothing about any of these countries. I cannot speak their languages, and it is, alas! necessary for me to have within reach a doctor who knows my constitution. Different latitudes demand different methods of medical treatment. If I listened to you, I should run the risk – '

Petresco sadly shook his head: 'Master, master, you ought not to say "if I listened to you . . ." because deep in your heart you have signed. Do you love your country? Do you love your fame? Then you must come. If you are sick it is I who will look after you. Over there are the most great doctors. Master, we *must* start away: I have already arranged all things, reserved the halls, ordered the bills – GUILLAUME FONTANE. . . . The ladies, they will be distraught when they read. And what ladies, master! They are the most pretty and the most loving in the world. I say to you, who am far from being the master, that over there I have known – '

Fontane raised an arm towards the topmost shelves where slept the philosophers.

'That is precisely what I do not want,' he said; 'I am no longer of an age to seek adventures, my friend.'

'No longer the age of adventures! Master, you have pos-it-ive-ly the age of adventures. Your great Colette have said: "at twenty years one does not seduce, one is seduced". But at fifty years . . .'

'Soon sixty,' sighed Fontane.

Ovid Petresco expressed the most flattering amazement:

'That is *not* possible!' he said with invincible authority.

This was pleasing to Fontane. Nevertheless, he stood out for a long time. But Petresco returned again and again with unwearied patience. One assault wave followed another, each of them carrying away some part of the defences. The American-Romanian became a familiar figure in the house. Alexis would say, with melancholy resignation, 'It's that gentleman again, sir. . . .' Madame Fontane called him the 'midget'. Fontane, enchanted by the visitor's Latin name, referred to him as 'Ovidius Naso'. Hervé Marcenat, who had been present at more than one of the Fontane–Petresco interchanges, put Pauline on her guard.

'If you let him come back, madame, Monsieur Fontane will end by signing. The *midget* is a force of nature. His curious speech sometimes conceals the working of his mind: but he is very subtle.'

'And why', she said, 'should Guillaume *not* set out to convert the penguins? It would be an amusement for him, and he would be all the readier to savour the pleasures of home when he comes back: "*L'un d'eux, s'ennuyant au logis*".'

'One of them? . . . Wouldn't you go too?'

'Certainly not!' she said with great determination. 'I have been at death's door: I need a long period of rest. Besides, the trip does not tempt me. I was only too glad, in the old days, to go with Guillaume to Italy, Greece, Egypt, but these new continents which have no past –'

'No past, madame! What about the Incas? What about the Mayas?'

'I don't like savage idols,' she said; 'they don't belong to *my* past.'

'Have you no fear, if you let Monsieur Fontane go alone, of the inevitable temptations? The women of those countries are said to be voluptuous and kind. Monsieur Fontane will be a "famous foreigner". His prestige will attract the birds.'

She laughed.

'I am not in the least afraid of that. His recent disappointment has proved to Guillaume that he is no longer of an age for that sort of thing. After all, he will be only for a very short period in each of the various cities. No woman would have the time in which to make a conquest of him, still less, a permanency. Even if I wanted to go with him, I could not. I am very much better now, thank heavens, but only as the result of a great deal of attention, and a strict régime. No, if Guillaume accepts this offer, I shall stay at home. I shall spend my time classifying a lot of documentary material here which has never been arranged, and in resting. After the agitation of these last years I need solitude and silence. I have asked friends of ours in New York about this Petresco man, and am told that he is honest and reliable. So . . .'

Fontane still hesitated. The Wanda episode had left him feeling restless and discontented. He had been ready to return to his wife on a great surge of tenderness and love. But she had done little to encourage him. Several times, in the course of their walks, he had tried to recover the tone of earlier, happier days. But she had brought him sharply down to earth by confining their talk to practical matters which, to Fontane, seemed trivial and uninteresting. He had become silent, and chewed the cud of his regrets.

'Baudelaire was right,' he said one day to Marcenat : 'a man can go without food for two days, but without poetry – never. I cannot endure this being silted up by the flat occurrences of every day. Fundamentally, we exist only by refusing to accept our environment. Total acceptance is death. The corpse may resign itself to being no other than it is, but *only* a corpse.'

Alexis came into the room with a pained look :

'It's that gentleman again, asking to see you, sir.'

Fontane seemed sunk in thought.

'Ah ! yes,' he said. 'Ovidius Naso. Who knows but that

66

he may be the temporary solution. My friend, we construct for ourselves, in the course of fifty or sixty years, a carapace of duties, engagements, and constraints, which eventually becomes too heavy for us to bear. I am bowed to the ground by mine. Lobsters take refuge, from time to time, in some cranny of the rocks where they make a new suit of armour for themselves. That, no doubt, is the metamorphosis or sloughing off of the old skin of which I stand in need. Ovidius Naso is, perhaps, the Angel of the Lord. Alexis, ask the messenger of the gods to come to me in here.'

Alexis shook his head with a pitying air, and left the room with stealthy tread.

That day, Fontane signed, without reading, the contract presented to him by Petresco. He undertook to spend six weeks in South America, fifteen days in the United States, and to leave France at the beginning of August. That would leave him only a very short time in which to prepare his lectures. What should he talk about?

'The most modern subjects,' Petresco advised him.

'What do you call *modern*, my friend? That raises a problem. According to certain young men, I am not modern at all.'

'But, master, you are eternal!' said Petresco. 'Your subjects? Over there they like what has the new look. Talk about existentialism or talk about you. It does not really have any importance. If I put upon the bills – GUILLAUME FONTANE, without any titles, the ladies, they run to the theatre. A triumph, master: it will be a triumph!'

Pauline received his decision without a murmur, and even with a certain feeling of relief. She at once began to worry about differences of climate, and spent her time in collecting the necessary clothing. Petresco would accompany the 'master' in order to keep a watchful eye on him, and to organize the tour. Hervé Marcenat went with the

Fontanes as far as Bordeaux where the two pilgrims were to take ship. Fontane, he thought, showed signs of emotional disturbance, and appeared to be rather unhappy. It was as though he *wanted* a tearful scene of parting, and one last chance of abandoning the whole project. Madame Fontane, however, went out of her way to avoid being left alone with her husband. Only when the moment came for him to mount the gangway did she let herself be embraced, and even then, she remained curiously calm. From the dockside she called up to him:

'Are you sure you've got all your fountain-pens, Guillaume? – your two pairs of spectacles and your passport?'

Leaning on the rail, he made a slight gesture of impatience:

'Of course I have!' he called back. 'I've told you so three times already!'

Those were his last intelligible words. His final goodbyes were drowned in the blast of the ship's siren.

PART TWO

What have you succeeded in doing? In convincing me that I may still be an object of love? No; but in reawakening within me the daemon who tormented all my younger days, and in giving fresh life to those ancient sufferings.

CHATEAUBRIAND

I

WHEN, close on midnight, Guillaume Fontane entered the great hall of the Hotel Bolívar at Lima, he suddenly felt that he was at the end of his tether. For four weeks he had been moving from city to city, sometimes flying, sometimes travelling by train. In Brazil, as in the Argentine; in Uruguay, as in Chile, he had delivered lectures, addressed Press-conferences, and been received by Academies. As day followed day he felt more than ever how vain and foolish all this agitation was. At the beginning of the tour the warmth of his welcome had sustained him, as had the enthusiasm of Petresco, who never wearied of saying: 'A triumph, master! I said how it would be, a triumph!' Little by little, however, he had grown weary of the high-flown compliments, had begun to feel ashamed of being condemned, by reason of the multiplication of his public appearances, to repeat so many platitudinous remarks. But, worst of all, like a toothache which returns after a brief respite, the memory of his recent emotional crisis came back to torture him in his moments of solitude. 'Ah! Pauline, Pauline,' he thought, 'if only you had shown me greater tenderness, this would never have happened, and I should not have found myself an exile among strangers!'

To Petresco, who was translating the compliments of the hotel manager for his benefit, he muttered in an exhausted voice:

'Tell him, dear friend, that all I want is to be kept from visitors. Pomp and circumstance will be the death of me.'

'What pomp, master? Here, at Lima, you will be able to rest. We shall stay four days, and you have only two lectures to give.'

'And to how many presidents shall I have to be presented?'

'Only to one, master. Now – you must not be angry with me – you have to attend a Press-conference – just for five minutes!'

'But why, my good friend, why? So that they can say of me tomorrow morning in Lima what they have already said in Montevideo, Santiago, Valparaiso? What does it matter to us? "A ces vains ornements, je préfère la cendre." ...'

Petresco shook his head gloomily. This Frenchman did not have the serious outlook: it was impossible to understand what he said.

'It is necessary to receive the Press, master, because here it is enormously powerful. Only, in Lima, the journalists do not so well speak French as in Argentina.'

'What is to be done, then, my friend? I do not understand any Spanish – a serious fault on my part. If Corneille and Hugo had not known the language and the poetry of Spain, they would not have been what they were. Still, the fact remains that I do not.'

'I know, master, and have arranged for an interpreter – a young actress who made a tour for me last year. Very celebrated in the South America – Dolores García. You will like her, master, beautiful, charming: here she is!'

A young woman had just come into the hotel. She was fair-haired and hatless.

'She is indeed charming!' said Fontane. Her rather prominent cheek-bones hinted at Indian blood. The sea-green eyes, with their black-encircled pupils, were lively and caressing. Her warm smile had the attractiveness of youth.

'Qué tal, Lolita?' said Petresco, 'the señora Dolores García – the great master Fontane. At the moment you are entering this hotel, Lolita, the master – he is becoming ten years less old.'

72

'The poets are ageless,' said Dolores. She spoke French with so scarcely perceptible an accent that Fontane complimented her.

'And yet,' she said, with a happy laugh, 'I have never seen France nor Europe. But I was brought up in a French convent, Notre-Dame de Sion, and I am very fond of reading French books.'

'Indeed, and what books do you read?'

'Yours, *maestro*. But don't forget I am an actress, and that what I chiefly read are plays: Claudel, Lenormand, Giraudoux. I am always looking for plays to translate. But I read poetry, too: Laforgue, Valéry, Max Jacob, Apollinaire.'

'Not Racine, Musset, Baudelaire?'

'*Claro que sí* – here are your journalists.'

She went to meet them. Fontane was filled with admiration for her ease of manner. She came back in a moment and explained that three of the journalists were extremely intelligent critics with whom he would find it easy to talk, but that the fourth had a reputation for being –

She paused:

'*Cómo se dice?*'

'Difficult?' he suggested.

'Precisely, you will have to be careful with him.'

'Dear señora, you will be amazed at the flatulent inanity of my remarks.'

She laughed, and, as soon as the interview began, took it upon herself to see that it remained lively. Seated on a low chair, leaning forward and never missing a point, she gave Fontane the support of her presence through what was, for him, something of an ordeal. One of the journalists asked him whether, when he was writing a novel, he made use of real people.

'The answer to that question involves a species of mental chemistry which it is difficult to describe,' he said.

'The point of departure is real life, but the material supplied by the actual has to be – hm – digested and transformed by the artist into his own peculiar substance. Every character in a novel is a synthetic product. Tolstoy said: "I took Sophie, ground her up with Tania, and what emerged was Natasha." Goethe studied Goethe in order to make Werther, but Werther is quite different from Goethe, since, after all, it was not Werther who wrote *Werther*. Balzac and Stendhal might have happened to observe the same drama, but the result would have been two totally different novels.'

She translated this, then added, in French, for Fontane's ears alone:

'Much as a painter works? Nature employs a universal palette, but each painter has his own. We know that Marie Laurencin always uses the same pale blue, the same pink: that a picture by Greco will have unearthly greens and blues: that with Renoir, all the women will be – *cómo se dice?* – iridescent, like a rainbow?'

'Bravo,' said Fontane. 'But where the devil have you studied these painters if you have never been to Europe?'

'In books. I have reproductions.'

A rapid dialogue began between them. They had forgotten all about the journalists who kept their ears pricked, trying to catch a word here and there. Petresco, not liking this, broke in:

'Lolita, you must speak in Spanish. The master will have plenty of opportunity for talking to you again, but these gentlemen ...'

The 'difficult' member of the group now came into action. He asked a question, and Lolita snubbed him in Spanish. Then she said to Fontane, in French:

'The man's a fool! He has just asked whether you take us all for savages!'

'Tell him that, on the contrary, I know that your

74

civilization is one of the oldest in the world, and that it is my intention, in the course of this trip of mine, to make a study of your art.'

Dolores embarked on what amounted to a speech. She developed Fontane's remarks. He understood, vaguely, that she was speaking of the 'natural resources' of a country ready for poetic exploration – which he had not said. It gave him great pleasure to note the effect of her smiling gravity on the mulish countenance of the difficult one, who finally nodded his head in approval.

When the journalists had taken their leave, Petresco said:

'Ouf! Now the master must take some rest ... *Muchas gracias*, Lolita.'

'One moment,' said Fontane, 'one moment. First of all the señora García must take a drink with us to celebrate the happy issue of a conversation which, but for her, would have been an unequal struggle. What does one drink here, señora?'

'Call me Dolores please. I was baptized Maria de los Dolores, but everyone in this country knows me as Lolita. The local drink is *pizco* – I think you will like it, taken with ice-water.'

Over their drinks, Fontane and Dolores kept up an animated chatter.

'Tell me about Lima,' he said. 'What ought I to see here?'

'Everything! Lima is a mysterious and charming city. But you must not visit it *officially*. Let me take you *bajo del puente*, across the bridge, into the old Spanish quarters. You know that this used to be the seat of the Viceroy?'

'Certainly I do: the *Carrosse du Saint-Sacrement* is set in Lima. Can one see the house of La Périchole?'

'I will show it to you.'

'Are you La Périchole?'

'We have certain points in common. But she was gay, I am melancholy.'

'Not this evening!'

'No, this evening I am happy. *Soy feliz* – I do not know why. If I had a guitar I would sing you *flamenco* airs.'

'Recite some Spanish poetry for me.'

She passed her hand through her curly hair. He noticed that the fingers were long and delicate.

> *A mis soledades voy*
> *De mis soledades vengo*
> *Porque para andar conmigo*
> *Me bastan mis pensamientos ...*

'Which means?'

'"I go to my solitude – I come from my solitude – Because I need to have with me – Only my thoughts." It is by Lope de Vega. There are only two really great Spanish poets – Lope de Vega and Federico.'

'Federico?'

'Federico Garcí Lorca.'

'And Calderón?'

'He moves me less. He is a theologian. I adore Federico – I have played his *Bodas de sangre* here. Ever since he died I have had his portrait over my bed. Have you read his *Romancero gitan*? No? Oh! but you must. I will translate it for you. I have gypsy blood – did you know that? It gives me a tremendously strong will. You will see for yourself.'

'What a lot of things we must do together!' he said, 'walks, reading, translating, introspection.'

'If you would like that, *maestro*; a lot of things, indeed!'

She looked at him for a long time in silence. Petresco yawned.

76

'Master, this is not at all wise. You have had a very hard day, and it is after two o'clock. *Buenas noches, Lolita.*'

She rose to her feet with an air of regret :

'*Buenas noches, maestro,*' she said, in a tone of assured intimacy.

Fontane watched her leave them with a tripping step.

'What a charming young woman !' he said.

'Yes, a great actress, master. I took her as far as Mexico. The theatres, they were too small. ... *Buenas noches, maestro.*'

2

PETRESCO had organized a luncheon at the house of Don Hernando Tavarez, the president of the Lecture Committee. The French Chargé d'Affaires, a young bachelor, the baron de Saint-Astier, tall, pale, and melancholy, came with the Legation car to pick up the two men. The weather was warm, the sky overcast.

'This city has the most extraordinary climate in the world,' said Saint-Astier gloomily. 'For six months in the year a cloud hangs over Lima, covering it like a roof. It never rains. The French Professor who teaches geography at the University of San Marcos cannot make those of his students who have not travelled understand what rain is. They know the word. When the mist moistens the roads, the people of Lima say : "Did you see that rain ?" When the temperature goes down one degree, they sigh : "It is cold." In summer, for six months, the sun shines. At this very moment you would find it less than twenty miles from the city. It is sad, *cher maître*, that you will not have time for a visit to the Andes.'

'How many Indians there are in the streets,' said Fontane, looking at the crowds on the sidewalks.

'Yes, indeed! One half of the population of Peru is composed of pure-blooded Indians who still speak the *quechua*. They are wedded to the soil, to their herds of llamas. This is the University of San Marcos, *cher maître*, where you will be speaking this evening. It is the oldest university on the whole of the American continent, older than Harvard or William and Mary.'

'Do you know, Monsieur le Ministre, a young woman called Dolores García?' asked Fontane.

'I am not a Minister,' sighed Saint-Astier; 'merely Counsellor of Embassy and Chargé d'Affaires in the absence of my chief who is on leave in Paris. Lolita García? Who does not know Lolita? She does a great deal for us. She is always ready to recite poetry at our meetings of l'Alliance Française.'

'She is most attractive,' said Fontane.

'She has talent,' said Saint-Astier. 'Last week, on the square in front of the Church of San Francisco, she played in an *auto sacramental*, that is to say a Mystery Play: *El Viaje del alma* – *Le Voyage de l'âme* by Lope de Vega. It was very fine.'

'I can well believe it,' said Fontane.

The car entered one of the new quarters. Masses of bougainvilia, red and violet, swarmed over the white houses.

'We are now in the suburb of Miraflores,' explained Saint-Astier, 'where our host lives. You should notice, *cher maître*, how the new houses are built in a style reminiscent of Madrid, as you can see from the jutting wooden balconies and the wrought-iron screens before the windows, but also in the modern idiom which runs to great bare spaces of white stone, recalling, to some extent, Lyautey's Morocco.'

'Master,' said Petresco, 'Dolores García will be at Don Hernando's. I had her invited – especially for you.'

'Why for me?' said Fontane: 'for the delight of everybody.'

'I am much looking forward, *cher maître*, to hearing you this evening,' said Saint-Astier. 'Here, at a distance of more than six thousand miles from France, we have great need of visitors like you.'

'You do not seem to me to stand in need of pity. The ladies of Lima are very beautiful.'

'They have', said Saint-Astier, with a bored air, 'the largest eyes and the smallest feet in the world, but they are jealously guarded by their husbands. This is an essentially Catholic country with, among the Indians, some curious survivals of Sun-Worship. It is not, I can assure you, a bachelor's paradise. Here we are.'

Don Hernando came to meet them, an opulent and noble figure of a man. He introduced, in French, a couple from the Spanish Embassy, and two young women: Marita Miguez de Roca and Dolores García.

Fontane's face brightened.

'My Good Angel,' he said. 'She saved me yesterday evening from the lions to whom Ovidius Naso had thrown me.'

He gave an amusing account of his meeting with the journalists. At table, he found himself sitting between his hostess, who spoke only Spanish, and Dolores, with whom he conducted a long, confidential, affectionate, and familiar conversation.

'After luncheon,' she said in a low voice, 'do not let yourself be carried off by Saint-Astier or Ovid. I want to show you the old town.'

Fontane gave her a mischievous and understanding look.

'All right, then; I will detach myself.'

Then they joined in the general talk. Don Hernando, who was an historian, tried to explain to the guest of honour that there exists all over South America an undercurrent of hostility between the Indian and the Castilian elements.

'In Mexico,' he said, 'the Indian has triumphed over the Spaniard. Here, the struggle continues, and, for the moment, it is the old Spanish families who have the upper hand and supply Peru with a government. But since, in theory at least, we have universal suffrage, it is only too easy for demagogues to rouse the Indians.'

'Why *demagogues*?' asked Dolores, and there was a note of passion in her voice. 'Something has got to be done. The poor Indians are being exploited by the *haciendenos*.'

'*Momentito*,' said Tavarez, '*momentito*. The Spaniards of South America have always been slandered, Monsieur Fontane, because the earliest histories of the conquest were written by Anglo-Saxons. The Anglo-Saxons have solved the Indian problem by slaughtering the natives. *We* have preserved and converted them. Somebody should write a *Life of Pizarro* to show that the *conquistador*, far from being a cruel and treacherous man, very nearly became a victim to his faith in the Inca.'

'I am very ignorant,' said Fontane, humbly, 'but I seem to remember having been deeply moved by the story of that – hm – Atahualpa, who was thrown into prison when he trustingly went to what he understood was to be a friendly meeting. Is there not something, worthy of *Salammbô*, about his having had a room filled with gold by his subjects as a ransom for his life, after which, though the ransom had been paid, he was strangled by the *conquistador*?'

'You are very far from being ignorant, *maestro*,' said Dolores. 'That is the melancholy truth.'

'Are you interested in the Incas, *cher maître*?' asked Saint-Astier. 'If so, we must show you the Magdalena Museum.'

Dolores leaned towards Fontane: 'No!' she whispered. 'I will show it you!'

After luncheon, their host showed them his pictures.

'I must tell you, Monsieur Fontane, that, after the conquest, in the sixteenth and seventeenth centuries, a school of painting was established at Cuzco, the ancient capital of the Incas, in which many of the artists were Indians. They tried to imitate the Spanish paintings brought by the conquerors, but depicted incidents from the New Testament with local attributes – palms, bananas, pomegranates, and even their Sun-God. Since gold was very abundant in Peru, these artists used it to enrich their pictures even more than the Byzantines had done, as you can see for yourself.'

'Very interesting,' said Fontane: 'the costumes are those of the Incas, the colours are Greco's. But the general atmosphere is one of a very gloomy kind of mysticism.'

'Spanish art is gloomy,' said Dolores García, solemnly. 'Peru is not a gay country. This cloud which hangs over Lima, the volcanic landscape. Remember, *maestro*, that the Christ Jesus in our churches is often invoked by the name of "Nostro Señor del Terremoto" – Our Lord of the Earthquake. Nevertheless, there was an intermediate period – the Lima of the eighteenth century, the Lima of La Périchole.'

She stole a look at Fontane, and took his arm.

'Come and look at the water-colours of Pancho Fierro, *maestro*. Don Hernando has some delightful specimens. See, here are the *tapadas*, the women of eighteenth-century Lima, wearing mantillas which allow only one eye to be seen. Later, the Church suppressed that form of head-dress.'

'I see what the Church meant,' said Guillaume Fontane. 'There is nothing more provocative or more dangerous than a hidden eye!'

'There was, at that time,' said Don Hernando, 'regular riot among the *tapadas*, who demanded the right to resume the use of the mantilla. I rather think that they got their way. I have seen Lolita playing *Motin de las tapadas*. The costume was very becoming to her. Yes, indeed, you were irresistible, Lolita. But, then, of course, you always are!'

She noticed that their host's use of the second person singular had surprised Fontane.

'I don't think you realize, *maestro*, that in Spanish the second person singular is used as soon as people become friends. In two days, you will be using it all over Lima.'

When Fontane took his leave, Saint-Astier rose to his feet.

'If you will wait a few moments, *cher maître*, I will have the car brought round.'

'I wouldn't dream of it, Monsieur le Ministre, though I am most grateful for the offer. Don Hernando's luncheon demands the *mille passus post prandium*. Besides, walking is the only way to see a city properly. Perhaps this lovely Antigone', he added, turning to Dolores, 'will be so kind as to guide my doddering steps and my ignorance?'

'With pleasure,' said Dolores.

'And I, too, will walk,' Petresco announced firmly.

'No, my good friend, no. You have the last-minute arrangements for this evening to make. Do not worry about us. When we feel tired, we will take a taxi.'

The others exchanged glances, but no one dared protest.

3

THE taxi which took Dolores García and Guillaume Fontane towards the city was driven at such a pace that the young woman was constantly being thrown against her companion. This was a great source of amusement.

'The chauffeurs of Lima', she said, 'consider it a point of honour to drive dangerously. In one of the public squares there is the statue of an admiral who was knocked down ten times!'

'How oriental this street is!' said Fontane. 'The open booths are just like those one sees in Cairo or Marrakesh *souk.*'

'*Claro que sí.* Spain has left here many traces of Moorish and Arabic influence. And the other Orient, that of China and India, must have brought, in very ancient times, seedlings which have taken root. Do you know our *flamenco* songs? No? They are as much Arab as Andalusian.'

She leaned towards him and began to sing a sad air in a low voice. The harsh intonation delighted him. The look in her eyes seemed to say that the words were addressed to him. He asked what they meant.

'It is a declaration of love, violent and – *cómo se dice?* – lewd. *Es bonito, no?*'

'*Bonito*, yes, but tragic.'

'Yes, indeed,' she said, 'but love is tragic. For us, to sing is to weep. Our songs have in them both cries and groans. In them, the Virgin is called Notre-Dame des Angoisses, Notre-Dame des Sept-Épées, Notre-Dame des Douleurs. The Arabs have transmitted to them their monotony, their infinite patience, and the gypsies, a new and – *cómo se dice?* – profound note. ... I am gypsy to the depth of my being!'

When they reached the old Plaza de Toros, she stopped the taxi.

'From here we will walk. I want to show you the little old chapel where the torero kneels before killing or being killed. Do you love the corridas, *maestro? No?* – I will make you. But first it is necessary to love death. We Spaniards are always thinking about our deaths. We wish them to be lovely and honourable. What delights us in the bullfight is the spectacle of smiling grace confronting the murderous horns. ... *Nuestras vidas son los rios – Que van dar a la mar – Que es el morir.* ... You understand? Our lives are the streams – which leap into the sea – which is death.'

'Which is *dying*,' he corrected her. 'That is better. Who is the author? Your dear Federico?'

'No, somebody much older, Jorge Manrique. But death is in all our poets. A Spaniard lives only for his death. That is why the Americans go wrong when they try to teach us to live well. We do not want to live well – only to die well. Come this way, by the Alemeda de los Descalzos which leads to the Monastery of the Barefoot Monks.'

She had taken Fontane by the arm, and now broke into a dance-step.

'These statues under the trees', he said, 'remind me of our Luxembourg Gardens, which I very much hope to show you one day. Fundamentally, we French are classicists, and you – hm – romantics.'

'No,' she replied, 'it would be truer to say that we are people of the Middle Ages. We have no sense of proportion, we do not like it. Life is so short, and we want to savour it passionately, and, at the same time, fearfully, because we are risking eternal damnation; with hope, too, since a single second's repentance is enough to assure us of God's mercy.'

'You are a believer?' he asked.

She looked at him with surprise. 'How should I not be?'

Then she led him in the direction of the house of La Périchole. They had to pass through a poor quarter.

'Because of the earthquakes,' explained Dolores, 'these old houses were built with bamboo stakes, *canasta*, covered with plaster. Their roofs consist of thin planks, or even of painted tiles. A sort of city scene-painting. Even the church belfries are of *canasta*, but the silver images of the saints have cloaks of gold. Many, many Indians, *maestro*, died in the mines digging for those metals– and all in the name of a God who loves the poor, and was born in a stable. That strikes me as all wrong – does it not you?'

Freshly washed linen of many colours was hanging from the windows to dry. A blind beggar was playing on a mandolin.

'How curious,' said Fontane, 'to find the part played by beggars in Goya and Velázquez so exactly repeated here.'

'Beggars', she said, 'are a part of our life. To be a *caballero*, an *hidalgo*, has nothing to do with social position or the making of money, but with – *cómo se dice?* – natural generosity. In Calderón, the beggar goes straight to Heaven: the rich man and the hard worker find it more difficult to get there. Here we are at the Palace of La Périchole – that is what they call it here. Actually, it was the house of the all-powerful Viceroy, in which he kept his mistress.'

Fontane was amused by this example of Louis XV creole architecture, in which bamboos took the place of marble columns. The place had been turned into a barracks. In the courtyard soldiers were rubbing down their horses. The shod hoofs sounded loudly on the paving.

One or two men stopped in their work to look at Dolores García.

'*Mira*,' said one of them, '*es guapa*.'

She laughed happily:

'A somewhat crude way of saying that I am beautiful – the proper word would be *hermosa*.'

'It is the *formosa* of the Romans. If I spent a month with you, I should soon learn Spanish.'

'You will know it by tomorrow,' she said.

'So, *mira*, Guillaume,' (it was the first time she had called him by his name, and the impression made upon him was that of a caress) 'this is the room of La Périchole, with a canopied bed, and a lot of rather artless and voluptuous decoration. It was here that she entertained her lover. The chapel was next door, so that she might run into it immediately after committing sin, to ask pardon of The Lord. On this table is the gilded model of the *Carrosse du Saint-Sacrement*. . . . *Es bonito, no?*'

'*Mucho bonito*,' he said. 'I can imagine that what I hear is the stamping of Andalusian mules in the courtyard.'

'Look out of the window at that little trellised house in the fork of a tree. That was where the Viceroy took his siesta.'

'Charming eighteenth-century!' he said. 'Before the Great Fear fell upon the ruling-classes. Wonderful days, when the representative of the Catholic King could lodge his concubine under the same roof as himself without causing scandal! Alas! since our revolutions and our reactions we have turned moral: not in our hearts, where morality might have a certain beauty – but in our behaviour.'

'Ay! Guillaume,' she said, and once more took his arm.

As they left the palace, Fontane saw, in one of the booths, a number of rustic walking-sticks, and stopped to buy one. Mothers with their children in the avenue des Moines Déchaussés watched in amazement as he raised his stick to heaven, and, stopping dead, held a long conversation with Dolores, who was laughing. When they had been strolling for some time, she suggested that they should take another taxi to the Magdalena Museum.

'Would you like that, Guillaume? There is a wonderful collection of statues, potteries, and fabrics which tell the whole story of pre-Columbian civilization.'

'The art of the Incas? – most certainly I must visit the museum.'

'Not of the Incas, Guillaume. Everyone says that, because Pizarro and Almagro found Incas here. But they, too, were conquerors who, at that time, had only recently built their empire, after destroying a far older civilization, the vestiges of which you are going to see – four thousand years of art, as in Egypt – Ah! how happy I am to be the first to show you all this beauty. I am certain that you will love it.'

'So am I,' he said.

At that moment, the taxi swerved murderously, and Dolores laughingly clung to her companion's knee.

'It is a good thing', he thought, 'that my programme leaves me only three days in Lima. Things are getting dangerous!'

The museum enchanted him. He saw there vases as lovely as the best of those to be seen in Greece, archaic sculptures, golden ornaments. In baskets of wicker-work were the squatting bodies of the dead, buried with their weapons and their cloaks, the colours of which, deep green, dark blue, and garnet-red, put him in mind of Gauguin's palette.

'This visit', he said, as they left the building, 'has been a great experience. It is indeed thrilling to find in this continent, so completely cut off from our own and from

87

Africa, the very curves of Greek and Egyptian art. We have seen here, primitive vases, classic vases, realist and decadent vases – and, if the Conquistadors had not intervened, the cycle would have been begun over again. Do you fully understand, my beautiful friend, the grandeur of that eternal recurrence? Civilizations are destined not only to die: they are, turn and turn about, young, mature, old, and senile. The sweep of our own we cannot see at a single glance. Our inspiration flies off at a tangent. But when the whole panorama of these cyclical incarnations is unrolled for us, as here, in a few rooms, it presents an – hm – epic spectacle.'

'You liked it, Guillaume? Then I am happy. And now, alas! I must take you back to the Bolívar. Petresco must be prancing with impatience! But I should like to take you, just for a moment, into the little church of the Magdalena – it is my favourite.'

Fontane thought the tiny baroque church entrancing. The altars were surmounted by twisted columns of silver, supporting canopies. The opal-coloured glass of the windows diffused a pearly light. The Virgins and the saints were dressed like the figures in Murillo's pictures, but in real fabrics, real brocade. A woman, shaken by sobs, was praying with such fervour that she did not even notice the two who had just entered. Dolores kneeled down on the flags, and made a short prayer. Guillaume Fontane, watching her with admiration, felt himself transported into another, a poetic and passionate, world. The feeling came to him that something big, something beautiful had entered his life. A tide of happiness rose within him.

Dolores, her devotions ended, returned to her companion.

'Destiny,' she said in a low voice, and in a tone which was at once intimate and solemn, 'destiny is pushing us, step by step, into a great and unknown world.'

They stood for a few minutes motionless and silent, as though powerless to tear themselves from the beauty of the moment. When they reached the hotel, they found Petresco almost mad with anxiety.

'Master! master! what madness! Lolita, what have you been doing? The lecture begins in one hour. The master will not be able to speak . . . !'

But he was wrong. On that evening, Guillaume Fontane spoke better than he had done in the whole course of the tour.

4

AFTER the lecture, Saint-Astier invited Dolores, Marita, and a few young Peruvian writers to 'have one' at the Bolívar, with the result that Fontane got late to bed, happy in the knowledge of his success. He slept for several hours, and dreamed that he had heard Dolores and Pauline speaking of him in the friendliest fashion. Then Pauline, in the dream, had started to type, and the tapping of the keys woke him. Ovid Petresco was knocking at his door. Fontane got up and opened it.

'*Buenos días, maestro.* I make my excuses for waking you. I *had* to make sure that you would not disappear for the day, as you did before. Here you are not your own master; you are Guillaume Fontane; you are France. You are to lunch with the President of the Republic. Then, you have to go to the Alliance for a reception; and at six o'clock the Minister, Saint-Astier, he gives a cocktail for you in his private house. I tell you all this now, because Dolores has already telephoned to ask whether you can go out with her. I do not know what you have done to that woman, master! She says – never have I met so interesting a man. I am certain that, if you wish it, she is all yours. But today, master, you have duties. I make my excuses.'

He continued to treat Fontane with a mixture of affectionate adulation and pained severity.

'My good friend,' said Fontane, 'I am truly touched by what you say about this young woman, but I can assure you that I want neither her, nor any other. At my age, that sort of thing is no longer suitable. She might have a moment's madness, but she would quickly wake from her dream in an old man's arms. Then, the enchantment would be over, and I should suffer. You will, no doubt, tell me that the prize would be worth the suffering, but there is the suffering of others to be thought of. You do not know Madame Fontane very well: she is a wonderful woman, and I love her dearly. I have no intention of hurting her deeply, perhaps fatally, for the fine eyes, no matter how strong their power of attraction, belong to a gypsy with whom I have momentarily been thrown in contact.'

'Master,' replied Petresco, 'you must do as you wish. My contract with you is for lectures, not conquests, but if I were you I should gather the flowers that come my way. How can the señora Fontane know what you are doing in Lima? But *c'est votre* business, not mine. All I ask is that you will be ready to go to the President's palace at noon.'

'I shall be ready – and now please leave me to get on with my dressing.'

Scarcely had Petresco left the room, when the telephone rang. Fontane recognized the deep, throaty voice of Dolores García:

'*Buenos días, maestro.* I trust that you had pleasant dreams?'

'Extremely pleasant, Dolores: I dreamed of you.'

'Is that true? *Estoy contenta.* Listen, Guillaume: I have

just been speaking with your Ovidius. He explained that you were engaged for the whole day. But I want to see you again, and not in a crowd. You are going, are you not, at six, to the cocktail party at the house of the sad young man, the *Encargado de Negocios*? – *cómo se dice*? – the French Chargé d'Affaires? So am I. Could you not make your escape about eight or nine o'clock? We could leave together. I will have my car and could take you to dine at the Country Club: would that be agreeable?'

'It would be charming,' said Fontane. 'You shall sing me *flamenco* songs, you shall recite Spanish poetry, and you shall tell me the story of your life.'

'Do not let us make any programme,' she said: 'I like to look forward to the unexpected. Do not be too much bored among the great ones of this world. *Hasta siempre, amigo.*'

He remained plunged in thought. Why was she showing all this interest in him? No doubt, because he was a Frenchman, because for four days he happened to be the man of the moment, perhaps because she wanted to visit France. Whatever the reason, the fact was extremely satisfying. He found her infinitely more poetic and far fresher than any Wanda Nedjanine with her bits and pieces of Parisian snobbery.

The day seemed long to him. At the Presidential luncheon he met some Generals and Admirals with whom he exchanged compliments of the kind that are usual after a 14 July review. Their French vocabulary was limited, his own Spanish non-existent. The President, a charming and cultivated lawyer, asked him about the Constitution of 1875, about which he knew very little. He got himself out of the difficulty by telling a number of anecdotes about MacMahon, which were well received. At the Alliance, he made a speech on the necessity of protecting the French language, and adding to its renown. Saint-Astier's party, spangled with pretty women, was a rest. Dolores was there, very much alive, very much courted, but she spoke to him scarcely at all, and avoided whatever group of which he happened to be the centre.

'No doubt she is anxious that our intimacy shall not be generally remarked upon: a very proper precaution.'

Once or twice she sent him a wordless but friendly greeting from a distance. She had a curious way of puckering the top part of her nose, between the eyes, which appeared to mean: 'I *seem* to be a long way off, but really I am close to you. . . .' He kept a careful look-out for this signal, and replied absent-mindedly to the fair stranger who spoke to him about his lecture. As eight o'clock was approaching, Saint-Astier came up to him and said, in a low voice:

'I trust, *cher maître*, that you will do me the honour of staying on after the crowd has left. There will be a cold supper to which I have invited a few friends.'

'Alas!' said Fontane: 'I am extremely sorry, but I promised, this morning, to dine with Madame García.'

'With Lolita? I shall be happy if she will join us.'

'You are more than kind, Monsieur le Ministre – but I fear that is not possible. There are several important matters I wish to discuss with this young actress – a French tour, translations . . .'

Nettled, ruffled, and sore, Saint-Astier said in a lugubrious voice:

'It shall be as you wish, *mon cher maître*. . . . I am not a Minister.'

A moment later, Fontane nodded his head at Dolores, who replied with an affirmative frown. With artless caution, which deceived nobody, he waited until she had left the room before saying his good-byes. He found her outside the front-door. The house of the Chargé d'Affaires stood on the edge of an extensive olive-plantation – a surprising thing to find in the very heart of a city. The gnarled trunks were regularly spaced, the farthest being nearly out of sight. Their green leaves, lined with white which looked almost silver, gleamed softly in the light of the moon.

'This beauty has something Greek about it,' said Fontane. 'One might almost suppose it to be one of those antique groves where the poets wander, or one of those dark and melancholy woods where lovers meet in the Underworld. I have a feeling that if you and I were to penetrate into that blue-tinted orchard, we should forget the past and never again return to earth. Lethe must, surely, flow nearby – that river of kindly waters,' he added in a melancholy voice.

'Here is my small car,' she said, 'get in, Guillaume. The sad young man was sadder than ever this evening, didn't you think? The way his flowers were arranged was quite divine, yet there is no woman living in the house.'

'He was annoyed,' said Fontane, 'because I left his party in order to be with you. He wanted to keep us both to supper, but I did not mean to let anything in the world interfere with our little escapade.'

'*Querido*,' she said, laying her hand on one of Guillaume's.

She took the wheel, and started the engine.

The Country Club turned out to be a flower-decked hotel in the Hispano-Mauresque style of Miraflores. Dolores had reserved a table on the terrace. There were a few other guests. Fontane, sitting facing her, felt at peace; relaxed and happy.

'What would you like to eat?' he asked.

'Oh! I eat so little! My choice would be some underdone meat and a good French wine.'

He expected her to have Wanda's tastes in food. But

Wanda devoured steaks like a tigress, whereas Dolores, after two mouthfuls, left the rest of hers untouched, but drained glass after glass of Burgundy. Fontane asked her about her life, and she described the great *estancia* on which she had been born, the horses she rode bare-back, the catching of cattle with the lasso, a patio paved with mosaics where fountains played. Later, she had left home for the Convent. A very beautiful French nun had been fond of her, Sister Agnes, and had got her to play *Esther*, and this had determined her vocation for the stage.

'After that, I was always agog for the French touring companies which visited us. I had very little money, be-cause I was the youngest of a very large family, a sort of a Cinderella. A great Spanish actress who came here for a season, gave me lessons for nothing. She told me I had genius. Yes, that was the word the dear creature actually used! She begged me to devote my life to art. I've already told you that I have a – *cómo se dice?* – a will of iron. My mother, who had been left a widow, had plunged all of us into ruin by mismanagement of the estate. We had to find some way of making a living. So, I learned a great many parts and, at eighteen, tried my luck in the theatre. But, alas! I soon discovered that a woman, in the countries of South America, can do nothing without a 'protector'. A married man, not very young, but hand-some, provided the financial backing for the company. Oh! how I hate rich men, Guillaume! They lay traps for chastity, beauty, youth. They demand of us virtues which they do not practise themselves. Do you know the poems of Alfonsina Storni?'

'Who?'

'Alfonsina Storni. She is a great poetess of this conti-nent. She has suffered because of men and speaks of her sufferings in words of bitter beauty. Listen, Guillaume –'

She passed her long fingers through her hair, and recited with passion:

> Tu me quieres bianca,
> Tu me quieres casta,
> Tu me quieres nivea. . . .

'Translate, Lolita!'

'You wish me to be white – You wish me to be chaste
– You wish me to be snow – You, whose hand has held
many cups – You whose lips are smeared with many
fruits – You demand that I should be white (may God
forgive you!) – You demand that I should be chaste (may
God forgive you!) . . .

'It is a long poem, I will recite it all to you another day.
But this is the idea: Begin, you men, by cleansing yourselves of your own impurities, and then, as virtuous men,
you may insist that I be white, be snow, be chaste. *Bonito,
no?* I will give you the volume. I have it in the car. Poor
Alfonsina! Poor us!'

Resentment was making her tremble.

'And then?' asked Fontane, after a silence during
which she emptied her glass at one gulp.

'And then,' she said, 'I worked hard, and, in the long
run, I conquered. Suffering is the road to truth. I have
become such an actress as the men of the theatre need,
and have ceased to be a woman who needs men in order
to follow her profession. At the age of twenty-two, I
married an actor whom I had thought was great, though,
as it turned out, he was not even a man. Since then, I
have lived alone, for my art. Nothing has any importance
for me except the characters I interpret. So I have become
hard, and strong, and lonely. I have told you everything,
Guillaume, the good and the terrible. Do I frighten you?'

She looked at him, and threw back her head with a
smile.

'Frighten? I have never been happier,' he said.
'Order me a liqueur, will you?'
'A *fierce* liqueur?'
'*Sí.*'

5

WHEN they left their table, she took him into an empty room where a log fire was burning. They sat down in two armchairs set next to one another. Fontane could see their two faces reflected in a glass hanging on the wall, and was struck by the sudden youthfulness of his own. His eyes were bright, and a serene expression seemed to have effaced the deep lines at the corners of his mouth. He never afterwards remembered what he had said to Dolores at that stage of the evening, but perhaps it was that she was the very spirit of poetry. Whatever it was, she said nothing in reply but looked at him with an affectionate softness in which he could see both sadness and passion. Eventually, he, too, fell silent, and they sat, saying nothing, gazing into one another's eyes. From time to time she shook her head, as though saying 'no!' to herself, then let her eyes resume their former concentration. The fire crackled; the flames sang. Fontane felt as though he were in some place outside this world, in some sort of enchanted bubble, and could not even recollect what city this was. More than once, she opened her lips as though about to speak, but no words came. At last she leaned to him, and, with a smile, said, as though what she had to convey were very simple and quite unimportant:

'I think I love you.'

He was surprised, invaded by a torrential happiness, and, in spite of himself, after a momentary pause, murmured:

'I, also, love you.'

She closed her eyes, and said 'Ah!' as though she had suddenly been struck to the heart. Fontane heard in that 'Ah!' happiness, amazement, adoration, and suffering. 'What a great actress!' he thought. A waiter came into the room to look at the fire. Dolores, like somebody coming out of a trance, rose quickly from her chair:

'Let us have some air,' she said.

Outside, the moon had set. The stars were glittering in a blue-black sky. Fontane looked for the Southern Cross. She showed it him. They went back to the car, and got in. Before starting the engine, she turned and offered him her lips.

'*Como te quiero!*' she said.

They set off. Fontane thought: 'This is quite absurd, but exquisitely delicious.' He thought, too: 'The Spaniards say: "*Te quiero*" – "I want you" and not "I love you". Symbolic? He did not know where they were nor where they were going. Flower-filled gardens, a road bordered with gorse, then a beach, showed vaguely in the darkness. By the edge of the sea, Dolores stopped the car, and this time, they embraced for a long time. Then, she took his face between her hands, and said: 'I feel that my hands are holding all the happiness in the world.'

Deep down in him a barely audible voice murmured: 'Titania!'

'What are you thinking?' she asked.

'The eternal question addressed by every woman to every man!'

'Because men never speak their thoughts. I am entirely yours, but you are not mine – *nunca serás todo mío!*'

'How could I be all yours, Lolita? I am a man with a heavy load of memories. I have a country, a wife –'

'I forbid you to speak to me of your wife!' she said harshly.

97

But a moment later, she again flung herself into his arms.

'Sing me one of your Arab songs,' he said, 'in that voice of yours which gives to me both pain and pleasure.'

'They are not Arab; they are Andalusian. Listen.'

With her lips close to his lips, she sang, very low, in her throaty voice, with its excruciating dissonances. They stayed there for minutes or for hours. There was nothing to be heard but the soft, monotonous sound of the small waves.

'The sea's ironic mouth,' she murmured.

At last Fontane heaved a sigh:

'I am afraid I ought to go back. Ovidius Naso will be hunting for me all over the town.'

'Does he watch over you, even at night?'

'No, but he must have been uneasy at not finding me at the hotel. Besides, I have to make a speech tomorow.'

'Will you not be in better shape to do so after a night of love? I always am. I like to drive a hole in the night. But, if you insist, I shall drive you back.'

There was sadness, disappointment in her voice. When they drew up in front of the Bolívar, she laid her arm round Fontane's shoulders, and whispered:

'Would you like me to come up and say good night to you?'

He hesitated for an instant.

'Do not tempt me, *querida* (he shyly risked the word). You could never love me for long ... and then I should be jealous, unhappy. Besides, I have sworn to my wife –'

'Oh! your wife again!' she said irritably. '*Buenas noches, maestro.*'

He tried to embrace her, but she turned away her face. As soon as he had got out of the car, she drove off with sudden violence. As he passed the Reception Desk (with its keys hanging from innumerable hooks, it made him think of the ex-voto offerings in a baroque church) the Night Porter handed him a letter. He opened it in the hall.

It was from Pauline, a cold, almost impersonal, typewritten letter. It gave him a detailed account of what mail had come for him, described a dinner at the Larivières, and another at the Saint-Astiers: 'They told me that their son is Counsellor of Embassy in Peru: so, later on, I shall have news of your Lima lectures.'

'I hope to heaven', he thought, 'that the young man doesn't gossip! But what, after all, could he say? Nothing has happened, and nothing, alas! will happen.'

He went to bed as soon as he reached his room: but could not sleep. The whole evening passed before his eyes like a dream which had ended in nightmare. He could still feel the young and yielding body in his arms, the fair hair stroking his cheek, the tender mouth pressed to his. 'God!' he thought; 'what a fool I have been! If I had wanted it, she would have been here now, stretched beside me. She would be mine, and would be saying exciting things to me with all that gift of hers for mingling gentleness and tragedy. How could I have brought myself to renounce hours which would have been like nothing I have ever known!'

He remembered what a woman had once said to him: 'Only a fool does not gather rosebuds while he may!'

'And what for, in heaven's name? Out of loyalty to a wife who, I am pretty sure, attaches no importance whatever now to our sentimental life together. If I need proof of that it is here, in that icy letter she has written without one word of kindness in it from beginning to end, except for the final formula – and that is pure convention. Of course I love Pauline, but is it my fault that she has so completely changed? In what way, if it comes to that, should I be wronging her by spending with this divine creature one marvellous night which would have no sequel? After all, I am leaving in two days' time. Ah! how idiotic it is not to gather rosebuds!'

He felt feverish, and tossed and turned trying to find a cool spot in the stifling bed.

'"Gather ye rosebuds." What precisely does that mean? The single moment cannot exist in isolation. If once I had tasted these delights, I should want to have them again. Either I should return to this country, or I should arrange for Dolores to come to France. I should be in hot pursuit of this young woman of the theatre, up and down the world. But if I did that, Lolita, could you bear it? You like to make a hole in the night. Young men would be everywhere asking you to go dancing with them. A time would come, inevitably, when you would offer me your friendship, your affection; but, having known your love, I could not accept that poor substitute, whereas, now, what you have given me is an innocent dream which seems to have a value above rubies.'

Then he lashed himself. 'What cowardice,' he thought, 'this fear of suffering is! What simple courage, on the contrary, she has shown in offering me the gift of herself! But why did she do it? What can I mean to her? I am leaving here for ever the day after tomorrow. Does she really love me? – that is most unlikely – yet . . .'

He switched on the light and tried to read. Lolita had slipped into his pocket a small volume of verse. This he now fetched, opened at random, and was amazed to find that he could understand these Spanish poems without the slightest difficulty. 'Is this a gypsy miracle, or have I never really tried before?' The title of a sonnet caught his eye: *Reply of the Marquise to Certain Stanzas of Corneille.* What a strange coincidence!

> *Marquise, si mon visage*
> *A quelques traits un peu vieux,*
> *Souvenez-vous qu'à mon âge*
> *Vous ne vaudrez guère mieux. . . .*

The sonnet was beautiful, the theme bitter. 'You tell

100

me, great poet, that my beauty will pass, and that my name will be forgotten quickly if, in exchange for the immortal lines which sing of me, I do not accept a kiss from your old lips. Have you, then, so blind a faith in the long life of your verses?'

'*Un baiser de ta vieille bouche*,' he murmured, and felt a sudden horror of himself.

Je suis femme avant tout et le présent m'enchante;
Pardonne-moi si, plus qu'aux grands airs que tu chantes,
Je me plais aux baisers joueurs d'un jeune corps.

In giving him this breviary of disenchantment, he thought, Dolores had provided the cure with the disease. How she must have hated him at that moment! Would he see her again before he left for Bogotá? Tossing and turning, he composed a letter for her: '*Only because I admire you too much, have I dared to refuse you . . .*' But, no: any words implying that something offered had been refused would deeply offend her. Should he pretend that he had not understood? Or should he write nothing, and try to forget? But could he ever forget the hours they had spent together? Sleep did not come to him till dawn.

6

NEXT morning, a note from Petresco was brought to him with his coffee: 'Master, I waited for you tonight until two in the morning. I *must* see you because there has been an alterchangement in our programme. The Bogotá Committee have telephoned that I am desired immediately to discuss matters connected with the theatre. So I *have* to leave (alone) *today*, and the plane goes at six. I shall have three hours of sleep. You, master, will join me, as arranged, by air tomorrow morning. The Porter has your ticket, also passport, visa, and everything else. I *beg you*, master, not to let yourself be detained by *no matter what*. My reputation is engaged, the hall booked, the bills posted, and the seats sold in advance. Your second lecture in Lima is for half past six this afternoon, at the National Theatre. Hernando Tavarez knows about everything. Do not go to bed late because you have to leave the Hotel Bolívar tomorrow at five for the airport. If you do not leave then, I am dishonoured. Respectful greetings – Ovid Petresco.'

Fontane was much alarmed at the idea of travelling alone. He had never done so in France, where Pauline had always seen to tickets, formalities, and porters. 'Poor Pauline!' he sighed. 'So tyrannical, yet so indispensable!' Then he began to live over again in thought, the extraordinary evening of the previous day.

'Alas! there is no possible doubt: I am in love!'

Absurd though the idea seemed, he could not put it from him. Why had this marvellous young woman offered herself to an old man? Somewhat ingenuously, he looked at himself in the glass, and was surprised by the happy face which gazed back at him. 'Faust,' he thought: 'must I make a compact with the Devil? Too late. Yesterday evening, I committed the irreparable fault of refusing what I most desired in the world, and now I am leaving tomorrow. It is all over. *The sea's ironic mouth*, she said. How sweet her intimate way of addressing me.' At other moments, he thought: 'It is better like this. In any case, my going would have put an end to the enchantment. At least, I can go back to Pauline with a clear conscience...'

He was in his dressing-gown, and had just started to pack, when the telephone rang. Was it possible that she had understood and forgiven? He ran to the instrument. It was the French Legation.

'Monsieur Fontane? Just a moment. The Chargé d'
Affaires wishes to speak to you.'

He seemed to hear again the comic way in which Dolores had said: *El Señor Encargado de Negocios.* Then
Saint-Astier's voice spoke.

'*Mon cher maître*, I am told that your manager has left
Lima this morning. You are alone. Will you make up to
me for yesterday's supper by having luncheon with me?'

There was a brief pause, and then he added:

'I have asked Lolita García and a few friends.'

'Has she accepted?' asked Fontane with an audible
anxiety which must have sounded comic to young Saint-
Astier.

'Why should she not accept?' replied the diplomat in a
faintly ironical tone, 'seeing that I told her it was to be an
improvised affair in your honour? May I count on you?'

'Most certainly, Monsieur le Ministre: you are kindness itself.'

'Half past one, then, *mon cher maître*. .... I am *not* a
Minister.'

An extraordinary surge of happiness, mingled with
anxiety, flowed in on Guillaume Fontane. So she *had* con-
sented to see him again! But might it not be so as to give
her an opportunity to show how much she despised him?
'No matter,' he said to himself: 'the essential thing is that
I shall be able to enjoy that unparalleled charm once more.
Even her anger will be beautiful.' He spent the morning
reading what she had left with him. He thought the poems
remarkably fine, without being altogether sure whether
it was the poet, or the giver of the book, whom he was
admiring. At one o'clock he took a taxi, and was driven
once again, with feelings of deep emotion, along the road
which led to the olive-plantation.

Saint-Astier's party consisted of a Legation couple, very
'Foreign Office', the Rector of San Marcos and his wife,

Hernando Tavarez, and the attractive Marita. He was on tenterhooks because Dolores was not yet there. She arrived very late, giving as her excuse that she had been kept by visa formalities.

'A visa, Lolita? Are you leaving the country,' asked Tavarez.

'I have to go to Bogotá to produce the *auto sacramental* which we gave here. It has been in the wind for a month, and I got the telegram this morning. I shall take the early plane.'

'So shall I,' said Fontane, on a note of surprise, 'at six.'

'Yes, six a.m. How delightful, *maestro*, to have you as a travelling companion!' she said with perfect natural-ness.

'It is, indeed, a happy coincidence,' said Saint-Astier, without the quiver of an eyelid; 'we were slightly uneasy at the thought of Monsieur Fontane, who speaks no Span-ish, making the trip alone. You shall be his interpreter, Lolita; we put him in your hands.'

She made a faint curtsey:

'*Señor Encargado de Negocios*, I am yours to command.

' I am the easier in my mind, because Madame Fontane dined with my parents in Paris last week, and sent a mes-sage through them, asking me to keep an eye on his health. Our climate has not, I hope, *cher maître*, had any ill-effects upon your liver?'

'None at all,' said Fontane; 'I have never felt better.'

'Many of our papers have expressed surprise at your youthfulness,' said Tavarez: 'I don't know whether you have seen them?'

Lolita did not look at Fontane, but, on their way into luncheon, at which he was to sit beside her, he put a whis-pered question:

'You're not angry with me?'

It was a clumsy thing to say, as he felt even while he

104

pronounced the words. But she replied with what seemed to be genuine surprise:

'I? Why should I be angry with you, Guillaume?'

The luncheon was gay, and Fontane gave a brilliant account of his tour in Brazil and the Argentine. When the meal was over, Lolita, who, at the request of El Señor Encargado de Negocios, had brought her guitar, sang. Guillaume Fontane did not understand the words, but the look in her eyes seemed to imply that the songs were meant for him. Saint-Astier and Marita exchanged scarcely perceptible smiles, which Lolita noticed, but not Fontane. When the Rector and his wife had taken their leave, Saint-Astier offered to drive Fontane back to the Bolívar. He dared not refuse the offer.

'Till tomorrow morning, then,' he said to Dolores.

'Yes, indeed: six o'clock at the airport, unless you would prefer me to pick you up at the hotel?'

'Allow me, mon cher maître, to send the Legation car for you.'

'Many thanks, Monsieur le Ministre, I should be most grateful. I do not wish to complicate Madame García's departure.'

When he reached the hotel, he found three parcels, with a card from Dolores. They contained a woman's stirrup in silver, an antique piece designed with taste; the Collected Plays of Federico García Lorca; and a photograph of Lolita, swathed in veils, as a Wandering Spirit, on which she had written: For Guillaume Fontane, the compañera. He felt touched at the thought that in the preoccupation of departure she should have troubled to put together the three objects most likely to please him. 'She never mentioned this journey to me,' he reflected, while he struggled ineffectually to strap his bags: 'Did she invent it at the last moment so as to be able to go with me? Le Destin nous pousse, à petits coups, dans ce grand *monde inconnu!* She seems to be giving a definitely helping hand to Destiny! Why? What does she want of me?'

The Rector had spoken during luncheon of Quixote and Panza as representing the two eternal aspects of Spain. 'In me,' said Fontane to himself, 'there is a Sancho who mistrusts this miraculous adventure, and is afraid of being an old greybeard, a figure of fun in the eyes of the Melancholy Young Man, and still more afraid of what that young man will write in his letters home. But there is also the Romantic Knight-Errant, who gladly surrenders himself to the wind of passion which is carrying him away. Well, we shall see what we shall see. We are in God's hands!'

The time had come to go to the National Theatre. He found Tavarez there, Saint-Astier, and a fairly large audience. There was no sign of Lolita, but this was natural enough, since she had many things to see to. All the same, her absence depressed him, and it was the general impression that he spoke less well than on the previous occasion. He took his leave of Saint-Astier, who asked to be excused from seeing him off at the airport, owing to the earliness of the hour. He returned to the hotel to complete his packing. He was struggling with the silver stirrup which he found it difficult to fit into any of his suitcases, when the high-pitched trilling of the telephone made him start:

'Dolores,' he thought: 'to say she's not coming.'

It *was* Dolores.

'*Buenas noches, querido* – sleep well, and have pleasant dreams. All I want to say to you is – *Serás mío y soy tuya* – Can you understand, *no?*'

The miracle was that he did understand. She had already hung up.

'You will be mine, I am yours.' He had not come to this unexpected adventure with a light heart. After the Ned-

106

janine interlude, he had sworn that he would remain faithful to his wife: and now, here he was, accepting a dangerous and ambiguous situation, in which there was no room for complete sincerity. Did he want it? He no longer knew. 'We are in God's hands,' he thought again, and fell asleep.

7

THE airfield was still in darkness. The only things to be seen were the electric flares along the runways and the riding lights of a few scattered aeroplanes. An Indian porter took Fontane's bags, and uttered incomprehensible words. As yet there was no sign of Dolores.

'Bogotá,' he was repeating to the young man in a grey-blue uniform at the desk, when a hand was laid gently on his shoulder. The voice of Dolores was like a caress:

'*Buenos días*, Guillaume: can I help you?'

He at once left her to make all the necessary arrangements. The young men adorned with gold lace seemed to be so many page-boys waiting on her orders. The customs official never even looked at his luggage. The passport-control man saluted. The senior officer of the airport impressed upon the air-hostess the necessity of reserving two seats, side by side, behind the wings.

'You seem to be popular here,' said Fontane, 'though I confess that I am not surprised to find that you have miraculous powers.'

'They have all seen me,' she said, happily, 'in one or other of the parts I play. I get free seats for them, and this is their way of showing gratitude'; then, coming closer to him, and wrinkling her nose: 'Have you given up calling me *tu*?'

Nothing was changed between them. The loudspeaker

summoned the passengers for Quito, Cali, Bogotá. A moment later, he was seated beside her in the plane. The propellers roared. More than ever he had the feeling that he was in a dream. Was he really setting off for a honeymoon in the sky with a fairy? Behind them a couple from Lima, who knew Lolita, asked her about her journey. She introduced Guillaume to them. The woman had been to his lectures, and said:

'I recognized you at once!'

'Poor Guillaume!' murmured Dolores mischievously: 'You cannot even travel incognito! I am compromising you.' On the other side of the gangway a priest was reading his breviary, and, in spite of himself, glanced furtively at her.

'You are distracting his attention,' said Fontane.

'How am I going to distract *you*?'

'Me? I could look at you in silence for the rest of my life, and be perfectly happy.'

'Ah!'

It was what he called the *Ah* that 'strikes to the heart'. She corrected him: 'Te *regarder*,' and he apologized. She snuggled up against him.

'How much at home I feel!' she said. 'It is as though I had always known you.'

'Love', he said, 'creates, as if by magic, the memories of a wonderful past which has never existed.'

Behind them, the Lima couple were looking at them and whispering. Just as the plane left the ground Dolores crossed herself.

'I don't want to die *before* . . .' she said. 'At Bogotá we shall be in the same hotel, the Granada.'

'How do you know that?'

'I telephoned.'

'We might visit one another,' he said shyly.

She gave him a tender look.

'I am relying on that – not tonight, though, because we shall get in late, and shall be worn out; but tomorrow. Whatever you do, don't accept any invitation to an official dinner on *that* night. This time I should not forgive you. You must not defy me. I am a gypsy, and know some terrible spells.'

Her mobile face had suddenly assumed a tragic and menacing expression. He laughed.

'Do you really believe in things like that?'

'You must not laugh,' she said nervously. 'If ever you stop loving me – '

Then, without any transition she was again gay and caressing. She spoke of the plays in which she had acted:

'You can have no idea', she said, 'how a part transforms me. For a week, for a fortnight I *become* the character I am playing. When I was acting Benavente's Silvia in *Los intereses creados*, I felt, even off the stage, that I was a pure, sweet young girl. In your Giraudoux's *Tessa*, I was frivolous and melancholic: as *Yerma* I felt capable of killing. If you want me to become the woman you long for, write a part for me. From your flesh and your blood you will create a Lolita after your own heart, and I shall give life to her, for your sake. But the author to whom I feel closest is Federico, for he has realized that Spanish women are mothers rather than wives, mothers rather than lovers. What they long for is a son who, if necessary, will make vengeance certain. In their eyes the worst of all tragedies is barrenness. They cling to the fathers they have chosen for their children to be.'

Suddenly she seized Fontane's hand in an access of passion and drove her nails into the flesh.

'I should like a son by you, Guillaume!'

Fontane, amazed and not a little startled, made no reply. The sun rose. Through the porthole they could see a desert of pink sand, and, beyond it, the ocean.

'The moral code of your country', he said, after a somewhat long silence, 'is the joint product of the Moors and the Catholic Church. The Church is suspicious of pleasure, but loud in its praise of procreation. If the Lord is to be worshipped, there must be creatures to worship Him.'

'*Claro que sí*,' she said gravely. The temperature inside the aeroplane was rising. Dolores leaned her head on Fontane's shoulder, and went to sleep. He felt at once happy and embarrassed. The young priest glanced with surprise at this strange couple. Fontane could hear, behind them, the Peruvian pair, Dolores' friends, embark on a low-voiced discussion in Spanish, and, more than once, not without apprehension, caught his own name.

'I must', he thought, 'get rid of all trace of the social instinct, and just enjoy this marvellous sense of complete abandonment. What a strange woman she is, simple-minded, yet inspired.'

When, approaching Quito, the plane began to descend, she opened her eyes.

'You know Quito, *no*? That is a pity. I should like to show you the town.'

During the wait, several journalists, notified by Petresco, came to interview Fontane. Dolores acted as his interpreter.

'And who may you be?' they asked.

'What shall I say?' she asked him. 'Your secretary? your *compañera*?'

He raised his arms in a gesture.

'No, not that – tell them the truth; that we are not travelling together, that we met by chance in the plane, that you have been so very kind as to come to the help of a poor ignoramus who does not know Spanish.'

'Guillaume!' she said with a menacing wag of the finger. 'You are ashamed of me!'

'I am no such thing, but I am afraid of journalists. Suppose a hint of all this reached Paris!'

'You mean that if it were said that a young woman is in love with you, you would be dishonoured. That is what you are thinking, no? Your French friends must be very strange!'

She explained to the reporters that she was going to Bogotá on business of her own, and gave her name. There were murmurs of admiration.

'Dolores García! Why, we have applauded you a hundred times. . . . We did not recognize you. . . . Stage lighting is deceptive. . . . You are more beautiful close to than at a distance!'

They were more interested in her than in Fontane, and the rest of the wait passed in an animated conversation between the young men and the actress. When she got back into the plane, and sat down beside him, she helped him with his safety-belt, one half of which he could not find.

'Poor Guillaume! What would you do without me? Do you know what one of these boys had written? – *The beautiful actress who is giving a touch of loveliness to the autumn days of the novelist.* Fortunately, I saw it in time, and made him scratch it out. What would Paris have said? And what will Paris say if ever I go there? You must know, Guillaume, that that is my greatest wish. *Mira, querido.* I have thought so much about Paris, and have so often studied the map of the city that if I *do* go there, I shall not need a guide. Listen, my hotel will be in the Place Vendôme –'

'An admirable idea,' he said.

'When I go out of the hotel, I shall turn to the right into the rue de la Paix . . .'

'No, into the rue Castiglione, but you are not altogether wrong, because the one is a continuation of the other.'

Tu ne te trompes guère,' she corrected him. 'In that way I shall reach the rue de Rivoli. From there, by way of the arcades, opposite the Tuileries Gardens, I shall get to the Place de la Concorde. I shall see the Seine and the Champs-Élysées in the mild Spring sunshine. Perhaps I shall go to the Faubourg Saint-Honoré, to look at the shops. I shall want to do everything.'

'And at your side,' said he, 'there will be an elderly gentleman, very much in love, who will buy you everything.'

'He will *not* be elderly, Guillaume. I won't have you speak disrespectfully of my lover. He will have written a play for me in which I shall act at the Théâtre des Champs-Élysées, and, on the following day, I shall be famous through the length and breadth of Europe – *es bonito, no?* '

With such childish talk did they fill the time until they reached Cali, without their even noticing the equatorial heat which had plunged all the other passengers into a state of torpor. There they changed into a smaller aeroplane for Bogotá. The flight was beautiful but terrifying. The machine seemed almost to graze the peaks, slipping between rocky walls, crossing chains of mountains which became higher and higher.

'Bogotá stands at more than five thousand feet. The last time I was there I found it difficult to play exacting parts, because it was hard to breathe.'

When they landed, they found two groups waiting for them. One had come for Fontane, and consisted of Petresco, a Secretary of the French Embassy, and a representative of the Ministry of Foreign Affairs. The other was there to welcome Dolores García: Manoel Lopez, the manager of the theatre, several members of the company, and a number of dramatists, all of whom embraced her, and patted her on the back in friendly fashion.

'*Qué tal, Lolita?*'

Every now and then, a flash revealed the presence of a concealed photographer. Petresco, eager and fussing, organized a press-conference at the Granada, in spite of the protests of Fontane, who explained that he was completely worn out.

'Five minutes, master. Manoel Lopez, he will take us in his car – and will be the interpreter.'

'And what about Madame García?'

Ovid showed signs of impatience. He was bristling with reproaches.

'Lolita? Ah! master, master, do not worry any more about her. There are men here who will see that she is all right.'

This had the effect of arousing Fontane's anxiety. The young French Secretary was the bearer of invitations to luncheon and dinner next day, which was a Sunday. Fontane explained that he must have a day of complete rest, and begged that the ambassador should postpone the first reception until Monday evening.

'Ah! master, master!' sighed Ovid. 'I know what the complete rest will be!'

In the car, Manoel Lopez, who was a poet, recited Baudelaire. 'You will see,' Lolita had said, 'that in Colombia the talk is more of poetry than politics.' On this first evening, Fontane realized how true that was.

8

HE slept the sleep of extreme weariness, a deep and dreamless sleep. When he awoke, he felt light-hearted, stimulated by the sharp air. Outside, the church bells were ringing for Sunday Mass. He threw open the shutters, and saw a wide square, early morning crowds besieging the trams, and, across the roofs, an arena of high mountains streaked with violet clouds. His suite consisted of two rooms: a bedroom, simply furnished with a wide brass bedstead, a chest-of-drawers, an armchair: and a larger sitting-room with a writing-table and a big divan. His first thought was: 'Excellent! I can receive Dolores in my sitting-room without fear of scandal.'

But where was his 'companion'? He wanted to hear her voice, and looked at the time. She must be awake by now, but how should he find out? He lifted the telephone receiver and asked the hotel switchboard whether there was anyone who could speak French.

'*Francés?*' said a female voice. '*Momento.*' A man came to the instrument. Fontane asked whether Señora Dolores García was staying at the hotel, and whether they could ring her for him. He was told that she was occupying Room 19, and almost at once heard her sleepy and caressing voice.

'*Quién habla?* Oh, is it you, Guillaume? Yes, you woke me with a start – but that is as I should wish. I like to be wakened by your voice. Are you ready, *no?* Nor am I, far from it. I haven't a stitch on! Give me an hour to have my bath, unpack, and dress. When that is done, I will knock at your door. Do you hear all these bells, my love? *Bonito, no?* I must go to Mass, and you shall go with me. *Hasta pronto* – so long.'

An hour later there was a light knock at the door of his sitting-room. He opened it, and saw Dolores with a mantilla over her head. There was a fresh and roguish look on her face.

'May I come in for a moment?'

As soon as the door was shut, she threw herself into his arms.

'You are looking wonderful this morning,' she said;

114

'each day you look ten years younger. Now, we have to arrange our time. You are free?'

'*Je suis maître de moi comme de l'univers* – and more. But it was not easy to arrange. Ovidius Naso is very angry. He had a whole programme worked out for me. But then, he is not in love with you!'

'He would be, if I wanted it!' she said with a flash of white teeth. 'He had better be careful! So you *are* free. ... *Mira*, Guillaume. ... This is what I suggest. We will go to Mass together. Then, we will take a walk through the town, and lunch at Doña Marina's. It is not – *cómo se dice?* – exactly a restaurant ...'

'A tavern?'

'Yes, perhaps that is the word – a Spanish inn with a charming landlady. The artists, the poets, and the *toreros* eat there. Do not laugh! I won't have it! The *toreros* are poets. This afternoon there is to be a *corrida mano a mano*, which means with two *toreros* only. I was told yesterday evening that they are very good: two Spaniards. ... I should like you to take me there. Why are you pulling a face, my love?'

'I do not much like bulls, and was hoping to spend the day alone with you, here.'

'*Como te quiero!* Tonight, I promise you, we will be alone, but I am as eager to see a *corrida* with you, as I am to play Lorca for you. I have already told you that, for me, the *corrida* is a sensual pleasure, *no*? After dinner we will do what you like.'

It was sheer joy to walk with her through the streets. She clung to his arm, sketched a little dance-step, stopped before a shop-window, then forced her way through a gloomy, monastic crowd, all black mantillas and black skirts. The windows, with their pot-bellied iron grilles, were reminiscent of Lima and Seville. The surge of cars and pedestrians completely filled the narrow thoroughfares.

The men stared at Lolita. In the church, he was surprised to see her drop to her knees on the flagstones, and stay there prostrate. When she got up, he noticed that her eyes were filled with tears. Mass over, she went to say more prayers in the Lady Chapel, which was all gold and gewgaws, and insisted on touching a reliquary with some keys she took from her hand-bag.

'It is necessary', she said solemnly, 'to have the keys blessed, that they may open doors on to happiness, and salvation. Did you know that?'

Doña Marina was a Spaniard who had become an expatriate for reasons which were not very clear. She had the grand manner, and treated the foreign gentleman and the great actress quite simply as a loving couple, which Fontane found reassuring. 'I can't, then,' he thought, 'look too much like her father.' Lolita and she chatted away in Spanish so quickly that he could not catch a single word. At something said by the former, the landlady gave him an approving look, and spoke a few words to him.

'She says that you are a lucky man, but that I, too, have made a good choice.'

The Plaza de Toros was very like those of Spain. Long files of men and women were besieging the windows where the tickets were sold. Lolita led Fontane to where an official seated at a little distance was selling reserved seats at a very high price.

'I like to be low down,' she said, 'so as to see each gesture. The whole beauty is in the movements of the feet and the hips.'

She chose two seats on the shady side of the arena. Opposite, full in the sun, was a swarming crowd of the common folk, showing little patches of bright colours. A noisy band was playing dance-music. Beyond the arena could be seen the line of the mountains, rocky peaks separated by green slopes streaked with clouds which ranged from pink to violet. On one of the very highest points, paradoxical, unexpected, luminous, and airy, gleamed the white profile of a church.

'The Monserrate,' said Dolores.

When the *paseo*, surrounded by gendarmes, entered and went, with the traditional salutes to ask the President for the keys of the *toril*, she laid on Guillaume's hand one of her own which was trembling with excitement.

'Oh! how happy I am,' she said.

Fontane noticed with relief that there were no *picadors*. He would be spared the spectacle of disembowelled horses. This would make the *coup de grâce* more difficult, but the toreadors were good, and the bulls mediocre. A group of *aficionados*, on the sunny side, uttered collective and rhythmic cries. After the first bull had been disposed of, and the matadors made the round of the arena, saluting the assembled throng, several men threw their hats on to the sand. Lolita shouted her enthusiasm.

'If you had a pearl necklace, would you throw it to him?' said Fontane.

'Yes,' she answered, 'I adore courage.'

'And you feel no horror when the first gush of blood comes from the nostrils of the wretched beast?'

'Horror? I love it! Look at Rodríguez: how handsome he is with that hard profile!'

The second bull put up a better fight, and she cried out 'Bravo, *toro!*' She had started on a conversation with some of the occupants of the neighbouring seats, and they, realizing that she was an expert, passionately rejoined. All of a sudden, just as Rodríguez had killed his second bull (the third of the series), she laid her hand to her breast, and, in a choking voice, said:

'Take me away, Guillaume. I am not feeling well.'

He was frightened, got up from his seat, and gave her the support of his arm. A soldier opened a way for them through the crowd. When they were outside, in the empty, sun-drenched square, she leaned for a moment against a wall. Above her head the clouds in the full light of the sun looked like sudden flares of fire upon the Andes.

'Do not worry,' she said; 'it is nothing. It happened to me here once before. I think it is because of the altitude, and the dust in the arena, and the smell of the bulls. ....'

'But what is it, Lolita? Your heart?'

'No, not my heart. A sort of nervous asthma. I have a remedy for it, but I left it behind at the hotel. Call a taxi, *querido*, and drive me back quickly to the Granada.'

When they reached the hotel she seemed almost unable to draw her breath.

'Go to your room,' she said, 'and wait for me there. I will take some of my medicine and then come to you.'

9

TEN minutes later, she knocked at the door of his sitting-room. She was wearing slacks and a sky-blue sweater. Guillaume thought her more beautiful than ever, but she was walking with difficulty.

'Sit down on the divan,' she said; 'take me in your arms and tell me stories, or recite some poetry. This medicine of mine is very strong: it works violently, and I cannot speak. But I want to be close to you, and to listen when you talk.'

She lay in his arms like a sick child. Her eyes were shut. He did as she had asked, and recited poetry to her. The pieces he knew by heart were by Maynard, Ronsard,

Corneille, Racine, Baudelaire, and Verlaine. When he murmured:

Un je ne sais quel charme envers vous m'emporta

she opened her eyes and smiled at him.

'How good you are to me,' she said: 'I am not used to it, you know. Almost always, when I am ill, I am alone, and then it is terrible.'

By the end of the afternoon, the crisis seemed to be over.

'Do you never write poetry, Guillaume?' she asked.

'No, not now. I did when I was twenty, like everybody else, but it is not my natural form of expression.'

'I should like you to write some for me.'

'It would, I fear, be unworthy of you. Are you feeling like dinner?'

Much to his surprise, she said that she would go and dress, and that then they would go to the Temel, Bogotá's smart restaurant. She had just left the room, when Petresco burst in. He had come to tell Fontane of an excursion which had been planned for the next day.

'Your lecture, master, is at six. Manoel Lopez wants to drive us out to lunch at the Falls of Tequendama. You really must accept, master: they are superb, and these good people want to show you their country. They will be hurt if you refuse. I know all about this solitude of yours which is no solitude. Petresco, he is not a fool, nor blind. But the others, they do not know — not yet. For today I said tired from his journey, but tomorrow?'

'My dear friend,' said Fontane, 'I will gladly go if Madame García is included in the invitation.'

Petresco heaved a sigh, put on his air of injured innocence, and promised that Dolores should be asked.

'We leave at eleven, master. Would you be willing to dine this evening with –'

'All I want this evening', said Fontane with great determination, 'is to be left in peace.'

After Ovid had gone, he waited a long time for Dolores, and, since she did not come, went and knocked on her door. She was seated in an armchair, deep, it seemed, in a dream. Scattered objects of clothing lay all over the floor.

'Am I late, Guillaume? I am so sorry. Doing my hair made my heart beat too quickly: but I am ready: let us go.'

At the restaurant, she ordered, as usual, a steak and a 'good French wine', ate two mouthfuls of the meat, and emptied the bottle. Then she smoked innumerable cigarettes, in spite of Guillaume's protests. Tobacco, he said, was very bad for asthma.

'*Tesoro*, you must not try to make me live as you do, not as anyone else does. I am Lolita. I have always drunk and not eaten: I have always smoked. Not you, nor anybody, can change me. I love what I love, and I want what I love. I feel the need to live in a rather – *cómo se dice?* – diabolical way, knowing that I am in a state of sin on the very edge of damnation, but that the divine mercy is infinite, and that I shall most certainly be saved. Do you understand?'

'No, but I accept.'

He was in a hurry to return to the hotel, and answered her absent-mindedly. Ten times she lit a cigarette from the one she had just finished.

'Order me a liqueur, Guillaume; a fierce liqueur.'

'Darling, is that wise? It is late, and –'

'And you are in a hurry to get back, *no*?' she said, taking Guillaume's face between the palms of her two hands, without paying any attention to their neighbours. '*Querido*, the happiness to which one looks forward is far greater than the happiness one enjoys. You know that, *no*?'

She swallowed her liqueur at a gulp, in the Russian manner, then got up from her chair. The hotel was near-by. They walked back through the dark and narrow streets. In front of a door, she pointed out to him two tiny Indians, almost pygmies, who were lying on the steps, asleep, their sombreros fallen beside their faces which were the colour of terra-cotta.

'*Mira!* How much unhappiness there is in the world! Guillaume, you must write a play for me about Flora Tristan – a play of violence – and I will act in it.'

She had taken his arm, and was walking briskly, her heels making a clicking sound on the roadway. When they reached the hotel, he said, hesitantly:

'Are you too tired to come and see me for a moment?'

'For a moment!' she said. 'For the whole of the night! Go to your room – *Hasta pronto!*'

He thought: 'The die is cast!' After a short wait, he heard at his door the light taps which he already knew so well. She entered, wrapped in a fur cloak.

'How beautiful you are!' he said.

'Do I please you?'

He lifted her in his arms, carried her into the other room, and laid her on the bed.

'Why did you pretend that you were old, my love?'

'That was before I knew you.'

She was lying beside him, and he could not feed his eyes sufficiently upon her perfect curves. He praised the beauty of her breasts, her hips, her long legs.

'You are all I have ever dreamed, all for which I no longer dared to hope: poetry made woman, spirit and sen-suality conjoined. I love you in your moments of passion, and in your moments of repose.'

When he found some happy phrase in which to give

utterance to his praise of her, she emitted one of those 'Ah's!' which struck straight to his heart.

'Tell me more nice things,' she said.

She showed herself to be a bold lover, and more experienced than he had expected. That, too, pleased him. About two o'clock in the morning, he murmured:

'You ought to be going back to your room. You must get some sleep, and not risk being found on waking, here with me.'

She seemed to be vexed.

'Why? I should not care. Do you really want to send me away? I am so happy lying at your side.'

He fetched her slippers, her fur cloak, and held them out to her. She screwed her mouth into a sulky pout.

'It is not a lover whom I followed to Bogotá: it is a Cinderella!'

Then, she gave him her old adorable smile:

'*Buenas noches, mi señor*,' she said, and danced her way out.

When he was alone, Guillaume Fontane felt himself invaded by a sense of uneasiness. 'I am in love,' he thought, 'as I have never been since the days of my youth. What is going to be the end of it? In a few days' time, I am going to lose this woman. How touching she was, this afternoon, when she lay in my arms, scarcely able to breathe, and so trusting.' In this way his mind was set in a turmoil, but his body was appeased, and his heart was beating calmly, easily.

10

HE had promised Lolita to wake her at nine. The bells of Bogotá started him into wakefulness much earlier. A church clock, with a sweet and solemn note, struck seven.

He had not had much sleep, but, all the same, felt light, alert. 'Altitude?' he wondered; 'or happiness?' ... An old woman brought him his *desayuno*. At last he rang Room 19. A sleepy voice answered him. He could imagine Lolita, her eyes half shut, her hair spread round her on the pillow, lifting the receiver with her long fingers.

'Good morning, my love,' she said (this was becoming a rite). '*Es la voz de mi señor...*'

'What's that you are saying?'

'I said, "It is the voice of my lord." You are my lord, *no*? Have you slept well? You are not feeling too tired?'

'I have never felt better in my life.'

'You are astonishing!' she said.

After the ritual delay she came to his room, all ready to go out. Then they went down into the hall, Dolores two minutes after Guillaume. He had insisted on this little piece of play-acting. He met her at the bottom of the stairs, and said: '*Buenos días, señora*,' very loudly, for the benefit of the porter and the booking-clerk, neither of whom were listening. After a suitable delay, Petresco appeared, followed by Manoel Lopez, a handsome, dark-haired woman, and a strange man of about forty whom Lopez introduced as 'Pedro-Maria Castillo'. Dolores greeted him with many manifestations of friendship. Fontane looked suspiciously at this man with an intelligent face, a forehead from which the hair was receding, and an air of authority.

'Pedro-Maria', explained Dolores, with a considerable show of animation, 'is the best dramatic poet of Latin America. I acted in a play by him at Lima, but, until now, I have never met him. I am delighted to do so ... yes, delighted, Pedro-Maria! I have wanted to meet you for such a long time!'

Much to the surprise and anger of Fontane, she walked with great determination to Castillo's long American car.

Ovid Petresco followed her. Though Teresa Lopez was both charming and gay, Guillaume remained for some time perfectly silent. He was chewing over his mortification. 'Why did she do that?' he wondered. 'Doesn't she know that it was I who arranged for her to be invited?' Then, he told himself that, no doubt, she wanted to avoid creating any gossip.

'Tell me about Castillo,' he said to his companion. 'In France, poets rarely have Cadillacs.'

'In Colombia,' replied Teresa, 'it is not every poet who has a Cadillac, but everyone is a poet, including the owners of Cadillacs. My husband, Manoel, writes sonnets; my father has written a great deal of poetry; I, a little. Our friend Castillo is both a poet and a banker.'

'The bank explains the car,' said Manoel Lopez, who was sitting beside the chauffeur, and had overheard the conversation, 'the car, and much else besides. Pedro-Maria has a house filled with works of art.'

'And a lively taste in dancers,' added Teresa.

'I see,' said Fontane, 'he is Barnabooth.'

'No,' said Manoel, 'he is Castillo.'

The car had left the town, and Teresa pointed to the immense tawny plain which stretched unbroken before them, like a calm sea.

'Look,' she said, 'the Savanna.'

'It is like a lake.'

'It was a lake, once. According to an Indian legend, at the time when the Moon and the Sun were lovers, the Moon, one morning, woke and found herself jealous. Suddenly, in her resentment, she decided to kill all living creatures, and allowed the waters to form a great lake. This existed for several centuries, until a Jinn came and collected the waters together, and, by means of the falls, which we are on our way to see, emptied the lake, which became the Savanna.'

Teresa spoke an even purer French than Lolita.

'How does it come about that you all speak French as well as we do?'

'I was at the Sacré-Cœur, and Manoel at the French Lycée. Manoel wants to translate Valéry into Spanish.'

'Not the whole of Valéry,' said Manoel, turning his head; 'only *Le Cimetière marin*, and a few shorter pieces.'

The road began to run between high wooded slopes. The scene would have resembled certain Alpine landscapes but for the cactus plants which here and there struck an exotic note in the undergrowth. Suddenly, sheer walls of rock came into sight, and a precipitous canyon. The noise of the falls could be heard at some considerable distance, and very soon Fontane saw a wooden chalet standing in a thick wood, on the edge of a chasm.

'This is where we are going to lunch,' said Manoel, 'but first of all we must pay a visit to the falls.'

The second car, which had been all the time some two hundred yards behind them drew up alongside. Dolores, looking radiant, got out and went straight to Fontane. While still some distance from him, she wrinkled her nose in friendly fashion, and, at once, all the ill-humour which he had accumulated during the course of the drive evaporated. She took his arm, and led him towards a spray-splashed observation-platform.

'Come and look, Guillaume. It is very beautiful.'

Then, as soon as they had moved away from the rest of the party:

'*Como te quiero!*' she said.

The fall was like a living creature, spurting out great rockets of water on every side, which shot forward, ravelled out, came together in a thrusting point, then died away. It seemed a gigantic firework shot from Heaven to earth. The falling water was a pale, slightly golden, yellow, and the spray rising from the chasm formed a misty fringe of lilac-blue.

'There is a legend about this fall,' said Dolores, 'according to which it was born of the metamorphosis of a woman.'

'It has retained', said Fontane. 'all a woman's grace and madness.'

'Do you think that I am mad, my love?'

'The most graceful mad-woman in the world.'

The others joined them. Lopez took Fontane to see the inscription at the foot of the fall.

DIOS OMNIPOTENS
DADME LICENCIA DE VOLVER
A VER ESTA MARAVILLA DEL MUNDO

'You understand what it means, Monsieur Fontane?'

Turning to Dolores, Guillaume translated: '"Almighty God, permit me to come back and see again this marvel of the world."'

Everyone said 'Bravo!' Lolita wrinkled her nose, and Petresco, who was watching them, raised his eyes to heaven. Luncheon was very gay. Pedro-Maria Castillo knew no French, but Fontane, helped by the two ladies, tried to speak Spanish.

'We shall have to be careful,' said Dolores solemnly to Teresa; 'he will soon understand everything we say!'

Petresco gave the signal for departure. He insisted that Fontane should have at least an hour's rest before his lecture. Dolores suggested that Petresco should go in the Minister's car with Manoel, and that Fontane should sit between herself and Teresa in the Cadillac. The drive back was delightful. The two ladies sang, each in turn, and sometimes together. They played like two cats across the beaming Guillaume. But after their arrival, he grew gloomy again, when Dolores asked:

'What is your lecture to be about this evening?'

'It is the same one I delivered on the first occasion at Lima.'

'The one I have already heard? Then I shall take this opportunity of being with Pedro-Maria. He would not understand a word.'

They were standing by the car. She noticed that Fontane looked vexed, and took his arm.

'You must not look like that, *querido*. I must have a talk with Castillo. He is all-powerful in the theatre here. Come for me to the Granada as soon as the lecture is over. We will go and dine at Doña Marina's, and then return to the hotel together. Would you like that?'

'Of course I should,' he said with feigned good-humour.

He was feeling sad. While waiting for Lolita that morning, he had added two new passages to his lecture which, for her, would have had a concealed meaning. What should he do? Insist on her being present? There were too many watchful eyes. Besides, it was only natural that she should be concerned about her own career.

On leaving the theatre, he had the greatest difficulty in avoiding invitations to dinner. He managed to get out of them only by saying that he was not feeling well, and was in no mood for society. 'It is because of the altitude,' he was told on all sides, and each speaker had a special remedy to offer, a particular doctor to recommend. Finally he made his escape, dismissed Ovid who was uneasily dogging his footsteps, and returned alone to the Granada. As he was passing the entrance to the hotel bar, he caught a back-view of Lolita's slim elegance, and of Castillo's massive frame, perched on a couple of high stools. Surprised, and ill at ease, he drew closer and heard Lolita say in Spanish (which, unfortunately, he understood just well enough to make out the meaning of her words):

'I feel as though I had known you always, Pedro-Maria.'

Her voice was bright and happy. Hearing a footstep behind her, she turned and saw Fontane. She seemed neither surprised nor embarrassed.

'Ah! Guillaume,' she said in French. 'Did you speak well? I am sure you did. Won't you have a Martini?'

His voice sounded curt:

'Thank you, no. I shall go to my room and lie down. When you have finished your conversation with Señor Castillo, I should be obliged if you would let me know.'

II

As he made his way upstairs he suddenly felt that he had again become an old man. His mood had sharply changed, and he thought of himself as resembling one of those village squares which the gaiety of festival has transformed for a brief moment. But when the last fireworks are over, it resumes the poor and gloomy aspect of its every day, among the wreckage of dead suns. He was humiliated, ashamed, and angry. 'The very same words,' he told himself, 'and spoken in the very same tone. . . . Ah! what an actress! . . .'

He sat down in an armchair with its back to the door, and thought: 'It is all over! How could I ever have allowed myself to believe in so ridiculous a dream? Self-love is curiously strong!' Then: 'Well, so much the better. I can now forget the whole business, and return with a clear conscience to Pauline, who is the only spot of light left to me. A man can feel only a limited amount of love: and I was well on the way to squandering mine.'

For the first time since his arrival, he noticed the ugliness of his sitting-room. The furniture consisted of mere frames of wood covered with a sort of greenish army cloth. The only pictures were chromolithographs of the most trivial subjects. Until now he had scarcely even seen these things. 'Love', he thought, 'can bathe all things in its radiance, as Vermeer could touch his servant-girls with poetry. Then, the artist withdraws, and so does love. The servant-girl is once more a servant-girl, paradise a hotel bedroom, and Dolores García a coquette.'

He drew a painful sigh, then, in a spurt of anger, hammered the arm of the chair with his fist. 'How fantastic, once youth is over, to feel the sharp tooth of jealousy! This inability to resist. The voluptuous torment of the possessed!'

He tried in vain to read: 'Actress!' he said to himself. 'Actress!' At last he became aware of the familiar knocking at his door, and did not answer. The hinges creaked, but he did not turn his head.

'*Tesoro*,' said Lolita's voice, 'I have been to my room, and am quite ready. Shall we go to Doña Marina's?'

'As you wish,' he said in a weary voice: 'I am not hungry.'

'What is the matter, Guillaume? Are you ill?'

'Ill? No; merely disgusted with life, with you, with everything.'

'With me? Have you gone mad!'

She shut the door, came round to the front of the chair, sat down at his feet, and tried to take his hands, but he withdrew them.

'What is it, Guillaume? Is it because I was not at your lecture? But, my love, I had already heard it, at Lima, and I thought ...'

'It does indeed concern the lecture!' he said in tragic tones.

'But in what way? I have examined my conscience very carefully, and can find nothing with which to reproach myself.'

He shrugged:

'Indeed,' said he. 'What have you been doing since we parted?'

'Something quite, quite terrible, Guillaume! I went to the Club swimming-pool with Teresa and Castillo. Don't look like the Commander in *Don Juan*, darling, it was a perfectly natural thing for me to do, because I adore swimming – then, because the water was rather chilly, we went back to the bar of the Granada to warm ourselves with Martinis, and to wait for you. Then, Teresa went home. It would be difficult to imagine a more innocent way of spending the time!'

'Is it also innocent to say: "*Pedro-Maria, I feel as though I had known you always*"? Precisely the same words as you used to me: and since when have you used the second-person singular in addressing Barnabooth? You met him this morning for the first time!'

'What is that name you give him? . . . My poor Guillaume, in Spanish one uses the second person singular almost at first sight. I explained that to you. It is not even a sign of intimacy. The phrase which so shocked you is also perfectly natural. It is *true* that I feel I have always known him. I have read his poems: I know them by heart, and I have acted in his plays. Is not that a bond, *no*?'

In a tone of resigned and sad humility, she said, as she rose to her feet:

'Do you mean that everything is over between us, Guillaume? That you do not want me any more? That I had better go away?'

He, too, rose from his chair, half smiling in spite of himself:

'No, I do not want the death of the woman who sinned.

You have a right to two mouthfuls of red meat, and a bottle of red wine, before being cast into outer darkness!'

She took his hand:

'I don't want red meat; I don't want red wine. All I want is that you should love me. . . . Do you?'

He made no reply, and she said again:

'Guillaume, do you love me? Unless I know that you do, I shall go away.'

'Oh! what a mad creature you are! You know perfectly well that I do, only, you see, I am jealous.'

'I am glad,' she said. 'If you were not jealous you would not be in love. . . . *Soy feliz!*'

By the time they started for the restaurant they were again good friends, and Lolita's heels tapped gaily on the Bogotá cobbles. Doña Marina received them with a great show of affection. When Dolores had emptied her bottle and smoked a whole packet of cigarettes, she became melancholy and penitent.

'Guillaume,' she said solemnly, 'just now you were satisfied with my explanations, but they were false. You are right: I *did* play the coquette with Castillo.'

'You are always a coquette,' he said; 'there is no great harm in that, it is a form of good manners and humility.'

She insisted on making a full confession: 'Do not be too indulgent, Guillaume. I am not only a coquette, I am wicked and perverse. I am capable of laughing at those who love me, and of trying to hurt them, yes, even you. It is not my fault — I have been hardly treated by life! The first man I ever knew was egotistical. My husband, whom I wanted to love, perverted me. The result of all that has been to make me cruel. You, who have been nothing but gentle with me, I have betrayed — oh! in thought only, but that, in itself, is terrible!'

He began to grow alarmed, and indignant: 'What was it, then, that you said to that man? and why are you a coquette? A single, true emotion is such a lovely thing.'

At that moment, a violent revulsion took hold of her. With savage irony she mimicked him:

'A single, true emotion is such a lovely thing, eh? *Tu me quieres alba; Tu me quieres casta; Tu me quieres nivea*, that's it, isn't it? But I should dearly like, *buen hombre*, to see the letters you are writing to your wife! I have no doubt that you protest your love for her; that you say you cannot wait to be back with her; that you never mention the dangerous Périchole, so coquettish and so wicked, with whom, at this moment you are spending your days, and your nights! No? What right have *you* to preach to me about the virtue of fidelity?'

Fontane was filled with admiration of this tirade, which she had delivered superbly. 'What a great actress!' he thought again. He was not quite convinced about what she might have said to Castillo; not quite sure that she had not made him promises. But now, so close to him, and with the tears pouring down her cheeks, she seemed so beautiful that desire swept him free of anger. He remembered that it was late, that they were wasting precious time.

'Do you really want to come to my room for a moment?'

A look of triumph, veiled in tears, gleamed in Lolita's eyes.

'Order me another liqueur,' she said; 'and then we will go back.'

12

DOLORES spent all next morning at the theatre with the Director and the Producer. Fontane pacified Ovidius Naso by sensibly agreeing to lunch with a charming French

Ambassador who thanked him for the excellent effect of his visit; to dine at the house of the Minister for Foreign Affairs, a man of great culture, who treated him with marked affection; to speak on the National Radio, and to deliver a lecture on Paul Valéry which delighted this people of poets. By the time evening came, he was pleased with himself, and thought: 'Actually, it is the good Ovidius who is right. I am here to do a job, which is that of an elderly professor.' When Manoel Lopez said good night to him outside the theatre, he told him that the Minister sincerely hoped that he would pay a visit, next day, to the University of Medellín.

'You will not regret it, Monsieur Fontane. It is a short journey by air. You will be speaking to young people who have a passionate love of French books, plays, and films. It will be very useful for you and for your country. The only inconvenience is that it means getting up early. We will be at the hotel for you, with the car, at five o'clock.'

After a pause, he added:

'We have asked Dolores García to come with us. She is popular among the students.'

Manoel Lopez was a man of tact.

It was still dark when the men and Teresa Lopez met in the hall of the Granada. Castillo was one of the party, together with several Colombian writers. Only Dolores was missing. The Night Porter explained that he had seen her leaving the hotel on foot, about an hour before.

'I do not understand,' said Castillo, who was in a state of considerable agitation. 'It was arranged that I should drive her to the airport.'

Lopez looked at his watch, and said, in a tone of authority, that they must be starting. It was clear that Fontane was uneasy, but Teresa was able to reassure him. Dolores, she said, had spoken to her about this trip only the evening before. They would certainly find her at the airport.

But how would she get there? The whole thing was a mystery: Lolita loved mysteries. Sure enough, when the three cars reached the airfield, Lolita was already there and greeted them with an expression of considerable pride. To Castillo, who asked rather irritably what had happened, she replied with a somewhat muddled story, and then, drawing Fontane behind a column, murmured:

'Do not any longer say, my love, that I am a coquette. I can do a great deal for those I love. Listen: yesterday evening, Pedro-Maria spoke to me of this journey to Medellín, and suggested that he should come for me this morning, because there was no room for me in the Minister's car. I accepted, because it would be convenient. Then I thought that it would cause you pain, and that the jealous Guillaume would try to make something of what was really very innocent. So, I got up at four, and walked here. That was nice of me, *no*?'

Fontane felt confused and guilty. How unjust he had been in his summing up of that proud spirit! He had scarcely time in which to say so before the moment came for them all to get into the small aeroplane in which they were to make the journey. Dolores and Fontane, by tacit agreement, so arranged matters as not to sit together. Fontane had as neighbours a picturesque poet who amused him with his humour, and a clever but melancholy philosopher whom Lopez had introduced to him. Verses, sonnets, rondeaux made the round of the occupants. The cloudless sky was violet, and the outline of the mountains as sharp as in Greece. The acrobatics of their flight would have better suited a circus-performer than a pilot. Far below them the bright ribbon of the Magdalena showed distinctly.

'The journey by ship to Barranquilla', said Lopez, 'takes several days and is very picturesque. Stops are made at each town to take on freight and passengers. The captain delivers news and receives it. It is all rather evocative of the steamers on the Mississippi in the days of Mark Twain.'

The Rector and the Prefect were waiting for them at Medellín. The air, softer than that of Bogotá, was extraordinarily mild. In the countryside there was nothing to be seen but fields of flowers.

'We grow the finest orchids in the world,' said the Prefect.

There was an official reception at the University before the lecture, with champagne and speeches. Fontane could see Dolores at the back of the hall, seated between Castillo and Lopez. He went straight up to her, and said, in a low voice:

'You must wriggle your nose, or I shall refuse to utter a word.'

She laughed, and did as she was told with an expression of warm affection. Later, she thanked him for behaving as he had done:

'I love it when you are like that – young, ridiculous, and brazen. It made me very happy to think that you had left all those big-wigs just to come and speak to me.'

Between the lecture and the luncheon she expressed a wish to have a bathe in the hotel swimming-pool. Castillo and the Lopez couple had brought their bathing things. Fontane sat down in a deck-chair and watched the three of them. Reassured by Lolita's morning act of devotion, he was no longer jealous, but enjoyed the graceful movements of the water-sprites. Dolores, still wet, came and lay on the grass at his feet. Then she went into the club pavilion to dress. When she returned, she was smiling.

'In the club-house,' she said, 'there is only a thin partition between the men's dressing-rooms and the women's. Teresa and I were chatting all the time we were getting

dry, and Castillo shouted "I can hear naked voices!" ...
Es bonito, no?'

'I don't think it was in very good taste,' he said.

There was still half an hour before the meal, and she suggested that it would be a good way of getting warm to go together to see one of the orchid plantations. On their way back, they were caught in a storm, and Lolita's dress was reduced to the semblance of a damp rag. When she reached the hotel she had to borrow from the bathing-attendant a pair of linen trousers and a sailor's blue-and-white striped jersey. She arrived at the luncheon thus attired, with the trousers rolled high on her bare legs. This might well have shocked the Guests of Honour, but all of them, poets and officials alike, were charmed. This was Colombia where even High Functionaries were poets.

She had never been in better form. At table she established her intimacy with Fontane by her smiling asides. Castillo, sitting opposite, said in Spanish:

'I am watching a marvellously produced comedy.'

'What do you mean, a comedy? I have never been more sincere in my life!'

Castillo's smile was sceptical, and Fontane, for a fleeting moment, wondered whether her indignation had been assumed. What confidences had she made to this man? But his mind was quickly set at rest by the marvellous virtuosity which she displayed after the luncheon was over. Lopez had had a great fire of logs lit. She danced in the light of the flames, then asked for a guitar, and sang, afterwards reciting some very beautiful poems by Castillo, and this calmed the only critical member of the group. Then she crawled to Fontane's feet, murmuring incantations.

'Yes, yes, we all know you are a witch,' said Castillo to her; 'are you going to change us into swine?'

takes place in a cemetery. I have acted the part of Doña Ana, in Argentina. The verse is high-flown and rhetorical.'

'*Mira*, Lolita,' went on Teresa, 'Pedro-Maria thinks all those plays absurd, because Don Juan is represented, from the outset, as a mere vulgar womanizer. Had he been only that, says Castillo, he would have had neither the courage to risk eternal damnation, nor the strength of mind to be converted. The real tragedy of Don Juan is that he pursues the *mille e tre* because he has never found any woman capable of inspiring a grand passion. Do you understand?'

'What has *el señor Francés* to say to all that?'

'I think', said he, 'that it is a little too easy to interpret the need of ringing the changes – hm – on petticoats as a search for the Absolute. I find it difficult to believe that Doña Inez was the first woman worthy of love who came the way of your gallant. Besides, if the thousand and two others had been no more than common coquettes, where would the drama be? That a professional lover should have reached years of maturity without ever knowing the – hm – sublime of female passion, seems to me in the highest degree unlikely.'

He had freed himself from the arms of his companions in order to raise to heaven an imaginary stick.

'Guillaume believes in women,' Lolita explained to Teresa; 'that is nice of him, *no*? Do you know the poem by my dear Alfonsina on the subject of Don Juan, Teresa?'

Teresa did know it, and they recited it, taking alternate verses, and translating for the benefit of Fontane:

> *Noctámbulo mochuelo*
> *Per fortuna tu estás*
> *Bien dormido en el suelo*
> *Y no despertarás . . .*

Nocturnal owl – By good luck you are – Asleep in the earth – And will not wake up. . . .

'Why *by good luck*?' he asked.

'Because, if he did wake up, Guillaume, he would find himself living in our gloomy age. *Caballeros* without glory, without cloaks, without extravagance. I am a woman of Spain! *O extremada o nada!* All or nothing. Here we are at the inn, Guillaume.'

It was a huge shanty of plaited reeds standing beside the road, pleasingly rustic in appearance. Teresa pointed out, under a nearby shelter, a great primitive earthen oven in which innumerable Indian servant-girls were baking rolls of *yucca*. They had a sharp, salty taste. The tables of the inn were laid in the open air. It was much hotter here than in Bogotá. Fontane was surprised by the change.

'With us,' said Teresa, 'the climate is vertical. There are no seasons. When it is winter in Bogotá it is spring here, at Torca, and torrid summer at Barranquilla. Officially, tomorrow, 21 September, is the first day of spring, but that in no way changes the real seasons here and elsewhere.'

'What!' said Lolita, '21 September – but that is my birthday!'

'It is natural', said Fontane, 'that your birthday should announce the beginning of spring. It is a graceful legend.'

'No *despiertas*, Don Juan,' broke in Teresa. She ordered salt pork surrounded with giant bananas:

'You'll see,' she said: 'it is delicious.'

Already the two young women were nibbling away at scraps of grilled pork.

'*Mira*, Guillaume, all the young men at the other tables are looking at you with envy. They are thinking: "Two women for this foreigner! – that is too much."'

The meal proceeded in a continuous cascade of poetry, songs, and laughter.

14

THE lovely, solemn note of the clock sounded mournful to Fontane. It announced the beginning of his last day, the end of a dream which had belonged in some place outside time. He was due, next morning, to take the plane for the United States, where he would lecture for two weeks, after which he would return to France. He felt at odds with himself. He looked forward to being with Pauline again, with his friends, his books, and his work. At the same time, he sighed when he thought of the enchanted hours which he had so recently known.

'Never again!' he told himself.

He went through the morning routine without any feeling of pleasure, rang up Dolores, and then settled down to read his mail which a page-boy had just brought to him. There was a letter from Pauline. It was humorous in tone and, it seemed to him, ironical. At nine o'clock Lolita knocked, and then opened the door:

'May I come in for a moment? I don't want this last day to be overcast and gloomy, but I feel sad and depressed.'

'There is something', he said, 'I particularly want to do with you this morning. You said it is your birthday, and I should like to buy you a present to serve as a reminder of me. What would you like?'

Her face brightened. She threw her head back, and passed her hand through her hair.

'How kind you are, Guillaume! I have long wanted a large gold cross which I could wear round my neck, and I should love it to come from you. I saw some lovely ones yesterday in a jeweller's window in the Calle Real. Shall we go there together?'

They conscientiously went through the farce of not being seen in the hall together until five minutes had elapsed between their coming downstairs. Fontane, as he descended, thought: 'What a baffling creature she is! Belief with her is as natural a process as breathing, and she sees nothing odd in being given a sacred emblem by a transient lover. La Périchole! – but with more of tragic charm....'

When he saw her standing at the foot of the stairs, he felt tears in his eyes. 'Never again!' Then, for the benefit of the reception clerk – who was not listening – he said: '*Buenos días, señora.*'

Their walk through the streets, which were swarming with Indians, and noisy with '*Qué tal! Hombre!*', then their visit to the jeweller's shop dissipated their melancholy. Lolita chose a simple but massive cross, with no figure upon it. She put it round her neck immediately, and looked her thanks at Guillaume. When they were again in the street, she clung to his arm.

'I do so love living with you, Guillaume, going into shops with you, eating with you, never leaving you. Could you really not stay for another fortnight? – or even a week? The Rector of Medellín has asked you to talk to his students again. Do accept, and I will arrange to go with you. We could have two wonderful weeks there, *no?* One should never refuse a chance of happiness, *querido*: life is not so full of such opportunities.'

He was touched and tempted, but answered sadly:

'Gather the fruits of my old age? I am afraid that is impossible, Lolita. Petresco has booked definite dates for me in New York and Philadelphia. Besides, my wife is expecting me. I know you do not like me to talk of her, still – '

'You must not think that,' she said. 'Deep down I like

to know that you love and respect your wife. I may have shown a little petulance now and again, but I have a very much higher opinion of you for not saying, as most married men who run after me do say, that your home-life is unhappy. I will even tell you something which you may not know, and that is that you feel more admiration for your wife than you do for me. . . .'

'I admire her in a *different way* – and perhaps you are right when you say, *more*.'

'It is brave and honest of you to tell me that.'

He had to leave her in order to keep an official luncheon engagement, but she had been invited that evening to a farewell dinner given by Manoël Lopez and, as he put it, 'the poets of the Ministry'. The dinner was held at Doña Marina's in an atmosphere of friendship and melancholy. In the space of a few days a bond of affection had grown between Fontane and his hosts. The unusual presence of Dolores, far from shocking, charmed them. Sensitive to beauty and to talent, they were soon her slaves. Doña Marina had surpassed herself, and, after each course, vigorously took part in the conversation. As was but natural, a great deal of poetry was declaimed. Dolores obliged with *flamenco* songs, and it was close on midnight when 'the poets' took Fontane and his beloved back to the Granada. In the hall, for the benefit of the Night Porter, she said loudly:

'*Buenos noches, maestro.*' (Then, in a low voice: 'Would you like me to pay you a visit, or would you rather I left you to sleep?')

He shrugged:

'To sleep? Do you really think that I shall sleep?'

'Are you not Cinderella?'

She vanished with a smile, but, five minutes later, knocked at his door.

'I should like', she said, 'to spend these last hours in

143

your arms, just as I did on that day when I had my attack of asthma. Do you remember how sweet you were to me? This time it is my heart that cannot breathe – and that is an even worse illness.'

He switched off all the lights except one small lamp, sat down on the divan with Dolores stretched beside him, with her head upon his shoulder.

'Ay, Lolita,' she said, 'it is finished. No fine eyes, now, to look into mine, no pretty speeches to make my heart leap. May God bless you, my love, for all that you have given me!'

'I? I have given you nothing: it is you who have brought me everything. I have had with you the pleasure which demands words, and the pleasure which keeps silence. I have loved your laughter, and I have loved your tears. I have loved your madness, and I have loved your wisdom. To walk beside you, to go with you into a bookshop, to eat with you in an Indian restaurant – all has been for me enchantment. Ah! how I am going to miss you! My heart and my body will both be seeking you. Ay *Lolita!*'

He saw that there were tears in her eyes.

'You will soon forget me,' she said. 'The world to which you are going back is your world; there is no place in it for me. *Entras en tu mundo, querido, un mundo que yo desconozco.* ... I have gloomy forebodings, Guillaume'.

'You might as well say, Lolita, that I could forget the sweetness of the spring, the warmth of the sun, the thrill of pleasure.'

'Ah!' she said.

It was that 'Ah!' of hers which struck to his heart.

They stayed where they were for several hours, talking or dreaming. Lolita cried much, then, because he had asked her to, sang for him, in a low voice, his favourite song. How could they meet again? She wanted to go to Paris to

144

organize a season of Spanish plays. Fontane shook his head:

'In spite of your genius, there would be no public for you. Paris, born on an island in the Seine, is still an insular city. Besides, I should not be free. Here our love is innocent: it has harmed nobody. In Paris –'

'*Ay Lolita!*' she said.

He suggested a meeting in Spain. Could she not get an engagement in Madrid or Barcelona? He would go there at top speed. Alternatively, he would come back to South America. Ovidius Naso could arrange that.

The church clock measured out the night. When it struck four:

'Have you finished your packing?' she asked. 'Would you like me to help you? Have you got a book for the journey?'

'Yes: Stendhal: *La Chartreuse.* .... I bought it yesterday, because I feel more Stendhalian than ever before.'

'Because of me?'

'Because of you.'

'*Soy feliz.*'

When the packing was done, she went back into his arms. The solemn note of the clock roused them from their trance.

'Five o'clock!' she said: 'I must go down. Wait here for ten minutes. *Querido*, remember, I have let you see everything – the good in me, and the bad. But never forget that the only true thing in my life has been the fortnight I have spent with you.'

'And do not you forget. You have asked me to write a part for you. Here and now, I give you one: The Inconsolable.'

'Will it have a long run?' she asked, on the threshold of the door.

Then, with a smile, she vanished.

15

WHEN Fontane went downstairs with an escort of greedy, attentive boys carrying his luggage, he found Lolita already in conversation with Teresa. Lopez and Petresco came to meet him in the half-darkness of the hall, and greeted him in low voices and the affectionate and tragic mien of those officiating at a funeral. 'The awakening of the condemned,' he thought. The drive to the airfield was no less melancholy. Shreds of mist hung about the car. No one spoke. Even Lolita, as a rule so vividly alive, seemed to be in low spirits.

'Your visit, *maître*, has been an immense success,' said Lopez at last. 'We all hope that you will come back to Bogotá.'

'My dear friend,' said Fontane, 'if wishes can control events, I shall most certainly return.'

At the Control Tower, Petresco busied himself with tickets, Customs formalities, and money-changing. He had to stay on in Bogotá to settle the bills and to organize a number of future tours. Several Colombian writers, as well as a Secretary from the French Embassy, had put in an appearance, with the result that Fontane was compelled to play his part in an interminable exchange of compliments and thanks. Lolita had taken up a position in the group opposite him, and, from time to time, wrinkled her nose in a dejected manner. A little later, he managed to get close to her. She leaned forward, and whispered:

'Ay! Guillaume!'

Then the loudspeaker called the Señor Lopez to the telephone. Manoel hurried away and, on his return, said:

'It was the Minister. He asked whether this mist would

not delay the start of the flight, but the officials of the Company assured me that it would not. So, he is coming himself. That, for you, *maître*, should be a matter of pride. The Minister has never done such a thing for any of his foreign colleagues.'

Fontane looked at Lolita. 'Why the devil have I agreed to go?' he thought. 'I could have cabled New York postponing my lectures, and have gone with her to Medellín. What a benighted fool I have been!'

A long car drew up outside the Control Tower. Manoel Lopez hurried forward to meet his Minister. Three or four passengers, recognizing the occupant of the car, seized this heaven-sent opportunity of saluting so powerful a man. They were of the importunate species whom a politician cannot shake off, and, for a few moments, they monopolized him. Then he joined Fontane, and addressed to him a number of gracious words on the subject of his stay in their city.

'You, Madame García, are I know, staying on with us, and we are soon to have the good fortune of applauding you here.'

She spoke very eloquently to the Minister about her plans (almost too eloquently, thought Fontane, who liked to believe that she was prostrated by the grief of this parting). The minute-hand of the clock moved implacably forward. Only five minutes remained. Petresco drew Fontane aside to talk money-matters. Fontane, impatient at the interruption, said:

'All that does not really matter, my good friend. Let me say my farewells. I am sure that any arrangement you make will be right and proper. You can write to me in Paris.'

'Master, I must explain. Your ticket to Miami and New York, five hundred dollars, has been charged to you, but as a set-off to that – '

147

Fontane listened to no more. The loudspeaker was making an announcement: '*Los señores pasajeros para Barranquilla, Panama, Miami. . . .*'

The Minister took Fontane's hand and shook it in both of his with great warmth. The flashlights of the photographers showed up the look of distress on the traveller's face. Lopez, Petresco, and the other men slapped his back in friendly fashion.

'*Adiós, amigo!* Remember, you·have promised to come back.'

What could he say to Lolita, or she to him, in front of all that crowd? He went up to the young woman and laid a hand on her shoulder without a word. She closed her eyes, and her smile was very near to tears. Already the passengers were filing through the barrier.

'Master! master!' said Petresco, hurriedly thrusting into Fontane's hand a bundle of multi-coloured papers: 'Here is your tickets, the baggage check, the passport. . . . *Adiós, maestro,* and thank you. *Happy landing!*'

'Good-bye, my friend, and thank *you*,' rejoined Fontane, and joined the line of passengers. Just before entering the plane, he turned his head and saw Lolita, who sent him one last pathetic wrinkle of her nose. A moment later, he was in his seat and fastening his safety-belt with great difficulty. The hostess came along to help him. She was a dark American girl with a cheerful face.

'You must be a big shot,' she said: 'they sure made a fuss of you.'

But Fontane's English was so bad that she became discouraged. The propellers, one after the other, displayed their full torrential power.

When the machine was airborne, Fontane looked through the porthole. He saw the chasms and the peaks touched by the rising sun, and, very far below, in the plain, the silver ribbon of the Magdalena. He remembered, with a bitter sense of regret, the flight to Medellin. How young and happy he had felt. He opened the *Chartreuse* at random, and at once came upon a sentence which set him dreaming. It concerned Count Mosca: 'This Minister, in spite of his frivolous airs and his appearance, had not a temperament cast in the French mould: he did not know how to forget grief.' A harsh comment on the French! But was it true? Since the great storms of his youth, in the old Minnie days, he had had very few sentimental griefs to contend with. His life with Pauline, until recent months, had been happy and harmonious. Wanda had caused him a small amount of suffering, but in her case he had proved his possession of a temperament 'cast in the French mould', by quickly forgetting. This time, on the contrary, he believed that the wound was deep. 'Do I feel remorse? No. Have I, this morning, seen that sublime young woman for the last time?'

Fixed to the back of the seat in front of him was a large pocket containing a map, a menu, and a blank sheet of blue paper, intended for the recording of the traveller's chance thoughts and comments. He took a pencil from his pocket, laid the sheet of paper on the *Chartreuse*, and, almost unconsciously, began to write to the tune of one of the plaintive ballads which Lolita used to sing:

> Ce fut un jour mélancolique
> Que le jour où l'on se quitta,
> Par une brume symbolique
> Ay Lolita!

In this way he scribbled ten or twelve stanzas:

'I am reverting to the days of my adolescence! It is ridiculous, and delightful,' he thought.

'Please fasten your safety belts,' said the hostess. They were coming down at Barranquilla. On the sun-baked field, a prefect in white linen, who had been warned by

149

the Minister, pronounced words of welcome in Spanish. Fontane, who suddenly realized that he did not understand one single word of the language, thought: 'I have lost my beautiful interpreter.' These ten minutes of unintelligible talk seemed very long to him. When he got back to his seat, he took the sheet of blue paper from his pocket, and read through what he had written. 'Calf-love stuff,' he said to himself. 'Am I fated to be like one of those characters in a fairy-tale who have been transformed by a witch, yet remember what they once were?'

He tried to get on with the *Chartreuse*, but with each page his thoughts wandered to those sweet and glittering days through which he had been living. After a brooding pause, he found another sheet of paper, and, this time, wrote:

> Ô jours de bonheur!
> Ô grâce trop brève!
> Ce temps enchanteur
> Ne fût-il qu'un rêve?
>
> Sous ce ciel lointain,
> T'ai-je bien connu?
> Était-ce, au matin,
> L'or de ta voix nue?
>
> Cette douce image
> Où mon cœur se plaît,
> Fut-elle un mirage?
> Fut-elle un reflet?
>
> Ce jour de Torca,
> Une toile peinte?
> Ces pains de yucca
> Un songe? Une feinte?
>
> Au long d'un chemin
> De très pur délice,
> Je tenais la main
> De mon Eurydice.

Tendre Lolita,
N'étais-tu qu'une ombre?
Au royaume sombre,
Quel dieu t'emporta?

Et ce bel amour
Dont l'odeur m'enivre,
À ce mois si court,
Pourra-t-il survivre?

Having given form to his nostalgia, he felt at peace, and closed his eyes. After his sleepless night he quickly lost consciousness, and dreamed that he had reached New York and was in a vast hall where he was to lecture, and that, at the last moment, he had forgotten what he was expected to talk about. He woke with a start, in a state of panic. The pretty hostess was shaking him:

'My! you are a good sleeper!' she said. 'This is Panama.'

At Miami, he had to struggle with an implacable American Customs Official, over the silver stirrup.

'It is a present I was given in Peru. It has only a sentimental value.'

'Yeah?' said the man ironically. 'Sentimental, is it? But it's solid silver all right, and an antique. Sentimental silver, eh?'

Everything, at last, was settled satisfactorily.

16

DOLORES GARCÍA to GUILLAUME FONTANE

Hotel Granada, Bogotá

WITH eyes veiled in bitter grief, I watched you leave me, and suddenly the aeroplane swallowed you up. It was all over ! ... Gone the lovely expression in your eyes, gone the lovely things you used to say. I was suspended in space like a rain-cloud, soaked through with sadness and melancholy. I bit my lips very hard, and the pain kept me from collapsing in tears. I had to talk, to say silly, meaningless things. Fortunately, Manoel Lopez came to my help. He took my arm and, with a tact which I shall always remember, went with me to the car, where he spoke admirably of you. And now here I am, all alone in my room, alone with a feeling of deadly anguish, alone with my suffering. Perhaps I do wrong to write to you like this? But if I am suffering, it is because I love you, and I thank Heaven for letting me suffer. Your arm stretched out, your hand on my shoulder, and one last look laden with love. May God bless you, Guillaume, for all that you have given me.

Dolores

GUILLAUME FONTANE *to* DOLORES GARCÍA

Hôtel Pierre, New York

This morning I got your first letter, Lolita ! Ah ! what images did the mere sight of your writing conjure up ! I could see again your face, your small waist, and that little line between the brows which, even in a crowd, maintained an intimate and secret communication between us.

> À Lima, chez la Périchole,
> Je connus la compañera;
> Elle était belle, grave et folle.
> Le Seigneur nous pardonnera.
>
> À Bogota, par un beau soir,
> La señora se fit statue
> Si parfaite, hélas, qu'à la voir
> Toute ma sagesse s'est tue.

> Ah! que j'aimai cette piscine
> Où soudain, par un jeu nouveau,
> La sirène se fit ondine
> Et le corps entrevu plus beau
>
> Sortant des eaux, cheveux épars,
> L'ondine est devenue Méduse. . . .

Need I go on? – or is this unworthy of you and of me? How deeply I regret not having gone with you to spend two weeks at Medellín. You would have knocked at my door, and you would have said: 'May I stay with you for a moment?' In our rooms we should have had great armfuls of orchids, and I should have laid in a rich provision of memories for the winter. *Ay Lolita!*

DOLORES GARCÍA to GUILLAUME FONTANE

I have received your two letters, Guillaume, the one from the aeroplane, the other from New York. It is easy and simple to write. All the same, I feel that I have in my hands all the happiness of the world. Ever since you left, I had abandoned myself to sadness, but now your two letters have brought me hope. Does it please you to have accomplished that miracle? No? This divine visitation of words which come from your heart and enter by my eyes, this truth of a feeling which cannot be feigned, that is what your little sheets of paper tell me. I am going to confess something to you. By dint of reading and re-reading, I have come to learn your poems by heart. That may be childish, but it is true. *La sirène se fit ondine*. The whole scene is again before my eyes, and I am as though inundated by the beauty of that day. To think that it was all true! It is a rare privilege, Guillaume, to have lived such hours, and we were chosen for that blessing. *Hasta pronto, tesoro.* I exist because I love, and if you were hard with me I well might die. I look at my body embellished by that miracle, and I stroke my face because it belongs to you. Come now! I am going to take this letter to the post, and I am jealous of its destiny. Think of me as I think of you. That is all I ask.

Dolores

PS. Am I as charming as all that?

GUILLAUME FONTANE to DOLORES GARCÍA

> *Vous avez fait pour moi, chérie,*
> *Un été de Saint-Martin*
> *Si pur, que le soir de ma vie*
> *En est devenu le matin.*

> *Hélas! les roses de Septembre*
> *Aux premiers froids vont défleurir.*
> *Lolita, j'ai peur de décembre*
> *Et je voudrais ne plus vieillir.*

New York, 19 October: on a Sunday of loneliness, passionate dreaming, regret, and melancholy.

DOLORES GARCÍA to GUILLAUME FONTANE

I have covered alone the long desert route from Bogotá to Lima. I looked for you at my side. I had the impression that I was incarnating a suffering, unhappy, and prostrated character, who had not the right to express herself, and I tried to play it well, without affectation. I am sure you understand me. Now, here I am, back in Lima. Already, the sad young man has telephoned, and, after him, Hernando Tavarez, asking for news of your journey, and the charming Marita Miguez. How many persons and things here will make me think of you! Write, Guillaume, write letters *tiernas y enamoradas*, and remember that here, in this strange, mysterious town, there is a

woman whose life has been transformed by the miracle
of love.

Dolores

GUILLAUME FONTANE *to* DOLORES GARCÍA

I am leaving tomorrow for France, Lolita. My last lecture
took place, yesterday evening, at Philadelphia. I spoke of
Corneille. But, in point of fact, I spoke of us. Ah! if only
you had been there! True, you would not have been
present at the lecture. You would have found in Philadelphia some dramatic author no less powerful than his
Cadillac! But I am being spiteful, though my heart is full
of you. I have so loved your letters, '*tiernas y enamoradas*'. Your French is beautiful because it is simple. 'I
stroke my face because it belongs to you'. . . . How well
said that is. . . .

This evening, as on the occasion of our funereal vigil
at Bogotá, I have had to pack my bags. Alas! the fair head
no longer bears me company. From my window on the
twentieth floor, I see the changing traffic lights down on
the avenue, green lights, red lights; emeralds and rubies.
Do you still wear my golden cross, *querida?* Now, on
the eve of going back to a world which is so different
from the enchanted bubble in which we lived for two
whole weeks, I find myself echoing your thought: 'To
think that it was all true.' But that tiny point of light fills
all my universe.

PART THREE

*Open your neighbour's heart — which is your own —
but do not stop at the filth which is the treasured
content of every human heart. Dig deeper, and do not
stop until you have found innocence, necessity.*

I

Hervé Marcenat learned from the newspapers that Guillaume Fontane would arrive, on 27 October, by the *Île de France*. He rang up Madame Fontane and asked whether she would like him to go with her to Le Havre.

'Le Havre?' she said. 'What would be the point of that? There would be an odious crowd on the boat; I should scarcely be able to exchange a word with my husband. And then, the journey to Paris in a railway-carriage crammed with foreigners. No, I shall meet him at the Gare Saint-Lazare. That is the extent of my duty. Guillaume, I feel sure, will be delighted to see you there, too.'

The voice was cold and tired. Was that the tone of a woman about to see her husband again after so long an absence? Marcenat went to wait for the train at Saint-Lazare, and found Pauline Fontane sitting on a bench, nervy and exhausted. Standing in front of her, he spoke of the joy she must be feeling. She replied in carefully chosen words, and turned the conversation into other channels: Bertrand Schmitt's latest novel, Léon Laurent's dress-rehearsal, the new car she had at last obtained from Larivière to greet Guillaume's return. Her air of nervous tension made him feel embarrassed, and this feeling was eased only when the crowd stampeded towards the arrival platforms. The boat-train entered the station majestically. Hervé had difficulty in forcing a way for Madame Fontane. A tide of returning travellers surged down upon them. They had to move against the current. At last, he saw in the distance a man who was looking round him anxiously, and apostrophizing a porter with a stick raised to heaven. He ran to meet Fontane, and found him look-ing well, young, and tanned.

He piloted him in the direction of Pauline. Husband and wife embraced, and looked at one another with that inarticulate surprise which one feels when one sees again familiar faces after a long absence.

'You have got a little thinner, Pauline,' Fontane said affectionately. 'It was time I got back to look after you.'

'Yes,' she said; 'high time.'

'Ah! my dear friend,' said Fontane to Hervé, 'what an experience! Ovidius Naso had organized the tour superb-ly, magnificently! and what a continent! There lies the future of the human race. One finds in those lands the Latin tradition, garnished with a touch of the East, and rejuvenated by the American influence. And their French culture! Do you realize that the young women there know Laforgue, Max Jacob, and Apollinaire by heart!'

'There will be time enough later for your enthusiasm, Guillaume,' said Madame Fontane. 'For the moment you had better concentrate on getting through the Customs.'

The icy tone seemed to envelop the group in a cloud of constraint.

2

THE period immediately following this return was not, for the Fontane household, one of unhappiness or even hostility, but, rather, uneasiness and tension. Pauline was being only too obviously on her guard, and scrutinized, with her formidable gift of insight, her husband's every word and act. There was no lack of matter to arouse her suspicions. Guillaume Fontane had returned from his trip a new man. He spoke of South America with a rapturous enthusiasm which surprised, and, at times, shocked his friends.

'I am prepared to believe', said Edmée Larivière, 'that Bogotá is divine, but Guillaume has certainly never talked like that about Florence or Toledo!'

She noticed, too, that he discoursed with special pleasure on the subject of love, showing an authority charged with implications which amused his younger listeners. When he went to the Théâtre Français to see a revival of *Bérénice*, he wandered through the corridors, saying over and over again: 'There's beauty for you, say what you like – sheer beauty!' and declaiming:

> *Pour jamais! Ah! seigneur, songez-vous en vous-même*
> *Combien ce mot cruel est affreux quand on aime?*
> *Dans un mois, dans un an, comment souffrirons-nous*
> *Que le jour recommence et que le jour finisse*
> *Sans que jamais Titus puisse voir Bérénice . . .?*

It was but natural that he should praise what was, indeed, admirable, but why did he recite this tirade as though it were a personal confidence, as though he, Fontane, were the Titus for whom some Berenice, separated from him by '*tant de mers*', was weeping?

Pauline Fontane was far too observant not to grasp these shades of meaning. She noticed that her husband was always, in and out of season, singing the praises of fleshly love. 'No profound beauty without profound sensuality', became one of his favourite themes. He was now showing a passionate interest in Spanish literature, and exiled a hundred or so French books to the attics to make room on his shelves for Lope de Vega, Calderón, and Federico García Lorca. When he was asked what his next work was to be, he spoke of a species of drama on the subject of Abigail, the virgin of Sunam who had brought warmth to the old age of King David: sometimes, too, of

a *Faust*. But, most noticeable of all, was the impatience
with which he watched for the arrival of the postman, an
impatience which nothing could explain. Alexis, who had
never before seen him like this, expressed a melancholy
surprise.

'Why did monsieur ring for you?' asked Pauline.

'This is the *third time*, madame, that monsieur has
inquired whether the post has come yet!' said Alexis,
raising his eyes to heaven.

Edmée Larivière summoned Hervé Marcenat to the
Quai de Béthune, and questioned him.

'I suppose you know all about the way the Great Man
has been cavorting in the Antipodes?'

'What exactly do you mean?'

'Madame de Saint-Astier has shown me a letter she had
from her son who was Chargé d'Affaires at Lima when
Guillaume visited the city. It appears that he completely
succumbed to the charms of a fair actress whose name I
have forgotten. All I know is that she went with him
everywhere.'

'But, surely, that is not possible?'

'All the same, it is true!'

'I only hope that Madame Fontane doesn't get wind
of it!'

'I can scarely believe she doesn't know,' said Edmée.
'Too many people in Paris do. Diplomats are the most
confirmed chatterers in the world. They make it a point of
honour to be informed about everything that's going on.
They drop endless bricks – diplomatically, conscientiously, but always with great skill. Pauline, unfortunately,
now has only men friends. She has excluded a number of
women from her Sundays, and they are not likely to miss
this chance of getting their own back! Don't look so
tragic, dear boy! This latest adventure is very different
from the Nedjanine affair. Wanda, living in France as she

does, was a permanent temptation. The fair actress is at the other side of the world. I gather that she really is an adorable creature – and I can't help wondering', said Edmée with a dreamy look in her eyes, 'why she made this dead set at Guillaume.'

'He is an interesting and a famous man.'

'Agreed, but, after all, he is not far off sixty, and what use is he likely to be to an actress, since he does not write for the stage? No, I suppose it is all explained by the fact that for several weeks, over there, he was the lion of the season. We women, you know, always need something or someone to show us off to advantage – brilliant jewels or brilliant men. Why? Because we have only just emerged from the condition of slavery, and are not yet very sure of our position in the world. That is our Achilles heel. We always need reassurance, and only a bodyguard of men can soothe our fears.'

Hervé replied that many men, too, need an artificial background, that they run after decorations as women run after diamond necklaces, that many puerile, and male, ambitions can be explained in terms of an inferiority complex.

'That is different,' she said. 'An ambitious man wants to shine in his works, or, at least, because of them. What the woman looks for is reflected glory. Take, for example, the conquest of Guillaume by this Peruvian creature. I understand that she is a great actress, and generally recognized as such. That ought to be enough for her, but no, she has got to get her hands on the lion of the moment. It's not a very serious matter. Our Guillaume will get over this little heart-throb, and you may be quite sure that I shan't open Pauline's eyes!'

All the same, Hervé felt slightly irritated by the intrusive presence of a foreign woman in the life of his friend.

3

CONFIDENCES and women have this in common, that those we desire too much escape us, while those we dread consistently dog our heels. Hervé Marcenat was very far from wishing to be Guillaume's confidant in the matter of this new adventure, but, when they were alone together, he felt that the threat of a confession was hanging over him like a storm that will not break. To all appearances, the Neuilly house had resumed the ordered measure of its days. The ritual Sundays had started again, but Madame Fontane remained preoccupied and withdrawn, and her husband had not settled down to work.

One day, when young Marcenat had been lunching at the rue de la Ferme, and Pauline had left the room immediately after the meal, he felt that he could not escape for much longer having to play the role which filled him with such painful apprehension. With every word that Fontane uttered, the secret seemed to rise closer to the surface, and only his deliberate refusal to understand had, more than once, succeeded in driving it down again. But a moment came when Fontane could no longer resist the temptation:

'My dear friend, I simply must talk to you about something which is causing me deep anguish. The fact that I have to hold my tongue makes everything so much worse, and I know that *you* will not betray me. Here goes.'

He proceeded to give a full account of all that Hervé had already heard from Edmée Larivière: that he had made the acquaintance, on the Pacific coast, of the most charming woman imaginable; that she was the very embodiment of poetry; that she had accompanied him wherever he went. Unfortunately, since getting back to Paris, he had had no news of her, and had sought in vain for something that might account for her silence.

'She wrote to me, while I was in New York, the most delicious letters a man could hope to receive – delicious is not the right word, the most beautiful, the most moving, I should say : and now, nothing ! Is she afraid that my mail is spied upon? Has she written down my address wrongly? For my part, I send her, almost every day, the most ardent missives into which I insert, as Voltaire used to do, a few lines of poetry, because she seems to like it. ... They are clumsy efforts, I would go so far as to say that they are deplorable. I am not, alas! a poet in the technical meaning of the term, but they spring straight from my heart, like the *Chanson du roi Henri*. ... Read this one, for instance. ...'

With a mixture of repugnance and curiosity Hervé read :

COMPLAINTE DE CELUI QUI NE REÇOIT PLUS DE LETTRES

Quand finira notre misère?
Pas de bien longtemps, j'en ai peur!
En vain je guette le facteur.
Quand finira notre misère?

Quand finira notre folie?
Les temps sont durs, le ciel est noir.
Si jamais Lolita m'oublie,
Je perdrai mon dernier espoir.
Quand finira notre folie?

Quand finira ce long silence?
Un mot et je serai guéri,
Mais rien n'interrompt plus l'absence.
Une ombre passe sur Paris.
Quand finira ce lourd silence?

Hervé handed the sheet back to Fontane without a word. He was sympathetic, surprised, and embarrassed. Fontane folded the sheet and put it into an airmail envelope, which he stuck down.

'Come with me, my friend. We will go buy some stamps and entrust this poor poem to the aerial post – "the post of the clouds" – as she calls it. Yes, I cannot leave such letters to be posted by others. Pauline would lose no time in asking me who this Señora Doña Dolores García is. So, every two or three days, under some pretext or other, I carry a letter myself to the avenue de Neuilly. It makes a pleasant walk.'

They went together into the Bois, and walked beside the little Lac de Saint-James. The golden, tangled masses of autumn foliage surged upwards from the island. A swan glided slowly over the dark water, leaving a double track in its wake. Then they went through a pine-wood where the regularly planted trunks, and the mysterious shadows, reminded Fontane of the olive groves of Lima. He tried to describe them to Hervé.

'The pale leaves in the moonlight seemed to me to be bathed in a – hm – supernatural radiance. Ah! my friend, I lived in those few weeks more intensely than in all my previous existence. How can one measure the length of time past save by the number of the images it has left in us? Each day spent with Dolores is, in my memory, worth a year.'

Hervé spoke of the danger of giving way to such memories. Why continue with a correspondence which both distance and wisdom must condemn? Madame Fontane was bound, sooner or later, to discover this interchange of ardent letters. What would she do? Already, certain of her women acquaintances had got wind of this adventure, and were talking about it. Why not put a full stop to an intrigue which, no matter how delicious, could not last?

'I cannot but be astonished, *cher maître*, that one so sceptical as you should be prepared to wager his life, and the life of another, on so fragile a sentiment.'

'Fragile! do not count on that, my friend! That scepticism of mine, as you call it, cannot but strengthen my attachment. If life, as your beloved Constant thinks, is no more than a phantasm, without a future and without a past, then why, and to whom, should I sacrifice the possibility of happiness?'

'To that question I will reply with a passage from that same Benjamin: *"The great problem in life is the pain one causes, and the most ingenious metaphysic cannot justify a man in tearing to pieces the heart that loves him."* ...'

Fontane, touched on the quick, stopped dead, and raised his stick to heaven.

'Ah! that is very beautiful!' he said; 'and only too true. Beyond all doubt, nothing can justify the giving of pain. But when the choice lies between two hearts, one or the other of which must be torn in pieces, what then? How can one deliberately break with her to whom one owes the most perfect moments of life? No, my friend, those are not things one sacrifices unless one is compelled!'

'*Cher maître*, your sacrifice has already been made. It dates from the day on which you left her.'

'Do not believe that, either. We have sworn to meet again, and the means will be found. She may come to Spain on a theatrical tour, or I may go and lecture again in Latin America. Nothing is impossible, provided the will is there. Distance cannot kill so deep a feeling: it only strengthens and – hm – purifies it.'

'And Madame Fontane?'

'But, my friend, this has nothing to do with my wife. Not for the world do I want her to suffer. I have told Dolores that, and she understands. What is between us is on a very high level.'

The dead leaves sounded under their feet like rumpled silk, and this melancholy whisper reminded the young man of the first walk he had taken, a year ago, with this same companion, under these same trees. In those days, Guillaume had seemed to him both enigmatic and authoritative. He knew now that he was weak and transparent, and this knowledge made him love him the more.

4

EDMÉE LARIVIÈRE decided to give a dinner-party to celebrate Fontane's return. She had invited the Saint-Astiers, who wanted to have first-hand news of their son; the Bertrand Schmitts; the blustering journalist, Bertier, and, much to the surprise of Hervé Marcenat, and in obedience to a direct request made by Pauline Fontane, Wanda Nedjanine. Bertier greeted Fontane with friendly reproaches:

'*Mon cher maître*, you make me feel jealous. You have just covered more than eighteen thousand miles, and you look younger than when you left us. It's a positive scandal! You must have made a pact with the Prince of Darkness!'

'From my son's letters,' said Madame de Saint-Astier in her shrill voice, 'I gather that the whole of the American continent was surprised at Monsieur Fontane's youthfulness. I believe you met Geoffroy at Lima, *mon cher maître*?'

'I did, indeed, madame, and he was so kind as to arrange several interesting meetings for me, on the borders of a sacred wood ...'

'That is what he told us!' broke in Madame de Saint-Astier in a tone so heavily charged with insinuations that her husband grasped her arm in an attempt to call her to order.

'And how did you like those countries?' he asked Fontane.

'Guillaume thinks that Paradise lies on the Pacific coast,' said Pauline Fontane with bitterness. 'Am I not right, Guillaume?'

'I never said that, Pauline. I said that I found those countries charming. They would have delighted you, had you given me the pleasure of your company.'

Edmée took energetic steps to break up the group. Hervé found himself in a corner with Wanda.

'Tell me, Hervé, this Guillaume of yours! It was scarcely worth while snatching him from poor harmless me, just to hand him over to an enchantress who is a hundred times more dangerous.'

'Have you, too, then, heard this story?' said Marcenat.

'As a matter of fact,' she answered, 'I am doing a portrait of a young Chilian writer, Pablo Santo-Quevedo. He has had to take refuge in Europe for political reasons. I find him full of warmth and originality, in fact, very much a *person*. Over there, Pablo was the lover of a certain actress, Dolores something-or-other, whom Guillaume fell for and abducted. Would you believe it, abducted! Could anything be more childish?'

'And what does your Pablo say about the young woman in question?'

'Seeing that he loved her, he is scarcely a good judge. From what he tells me, I gather that she is a mass of charm, and has real genius as an actress. But he also says that she is about as dangerous as they're made. She has broken up more than one marriage, she tortured her own husband, and has sent several young men mad, and then left them, as she did Pablo when she had got sick of him. She seems perfectly capable of driving Guillaume into a divorce if she is really and truly set on having him.'

'Don't talk nonsense, Wanda. She's at the other end of the world, and why on earth *should* she want Guillaume?'

'How should I know, Hervé dear? It is Pablo's conviction that, should she decide to call Fontane back, he would throw up everything, and that, if she decides to come to Europe, she'll get the governments all over the world on their knees to serve her just so's she shall have a comfortable journey. Pablo is superstitious: he says this Dolores creature has got gypsy blood, that she can cast spells, weave charms, and all the rest of it. No man has ever been able to resist her, he says. Those are the claws, Hervé, into which you delivered your master after having saved him from me. A beautiful, hand-stitched job, I must say!'

After dinner, Pauline Fontane sat herself down on a sofa with Madame de Saint-Astier.

'I know that your son was very kind to Guillaume: please send him both our thanks.'

Madame de Saint-Astier coughed:

'Geoffroy rejoiced at Monsieur Fontane's success. Your husband's talent has done good service to our prestige. But – listen to me, my dear – I do so think that we women ought to stand by one another. Don't let him go back to those countries.'

'He has no intention of doing so. Why do you say that?'

'My dear, I hate gossip, and Geoffroy would never forgive me if he knew that I had repeated something which he has told me in confidence. But I think it my duty to warn you. Your husband was seen about, rather too much, in Lima with a woman friend of my son's who, incidentally, is the leading actress in that part of the world. Please don't think that I am insinuating anything. I am merely drawing your attention to a danger, that is all.'

Pauline assumed an air of smiling security.

'Don't be uneasy on my account. We have been married for twenty-five years. Guillaume enjoys the society of women. I refused to accompany him. He looked, as was perfectly natural, for an interpreter and a guide.'

'You do not know this woman! Geoffroy says she is an enchantress. My dear, always be suspicious of men of that age. I never let Hector travel alone! If I were in your place, I should have a word with my husband.'

At a little distance, Guillaume Fontane, the centre of a group of women, was discoursing on the Spanish theatre. Pauline, watching him, thought: 'Heavens! how happy he looks! Why should I submit to the sour tittle-tattle of that old fool?' But, all the same, what she had been told made her suffer.

5

GUILLAUME felt that his relations with his wife were, more and more, losing all character of trusting intimacy. It was Pauline whom he blamed for this change. It never occurred to him that she knew anything about Dolores, and he congratulated himself on the prudent manner in which he had concealed his passion.

Of the artless enthusiasm, though it revealed much, with which he talked of pre-Columbian art, of the Savanna, and the Andes; of his absurd and sudden taste for South Americans passing through Paris; of his really quite idiotic display during a recital of *flamenco* songs at the Théâtre des Champs-Élysées – he was blissfully unaware. So, he could not understand why it was that Pauline remained sunk in gloom, and heaved such deep sighs during the silent meals when they had no guests. He tried to pacify her, and loaded her with presents which he chose with affectionate care, though only with great difficulty could she produce the shadow of a smile when he gave them to her.

One Sunday afternoon, when a pale November sun had broken through the clouds, he suggested a walk round the Lac de Saint-James. She accepted. The trees had lost their autumn foliage, and the water was low.

'What a part this little lake has played in our lives!' he said. 'It has witnessed our happiness, and our moments of despair: it has known us in youth and age, in sickness and in health. It is almost possible to measure the state of our physical well-being by the time we take to walk round it.'

Pauline stopped under a willow, the branches of which were trailing in the water, and faced him.

'How is it with us now?' she said. 'Separated for ever, or still struggling to put up a pretence of happy domesticity?'

'I don't understand,' he stammered.

'Nor do I, Guillaume. I don't understand what it is you want. Have you, or have you not, a Peruvian mistress?'

Astounded and horror-stricken, he hesitated for a moment, looked at the sky, at the water, and then said slowly:

'Yes: during that trip of mine I met a woman with whom I fell deeply in love.'

'I am grateful to you for at least being honest with me. I had decided that, had you lied to me, I would leave you this evening.'

The violence of his emotion revealed to him, all of a

sudden, the extent to which he clung to Pauline. He felt as though life were slipping away from him. After a silence, they continued their walk, side by side, along the path which borders the lake.

'But how did you know?' he asked. 'I did my best –'

'Your best! The incredible things you said, your artless pride – what of them? You could not open your lips, Guillaume, without crying your love aloud for all to hear! Our friends have noticed it. You have made yourself a laughing-stock! Even if I had not been warned, I should have guessed.'

'Then you have been warned?'

'What a child you are!' she said. 'Have you reached your present age without having learned that everything gets known sooner or later, that hatred is for ever on the watch, and that every piece of bad news immediately finds a carrier? There are people whose only pleasure consists in causing pain. I had two anonymous letters from Bogotá, telling me that you had picked up a mistress. One of them contained some newspaper cuttings. I do not know Spanish, and I failed to understand all they said, but three photographs, taken in different places, showed you with the same young woman, each time in a different dress. That at least I did understand!'

He stopped and raised his stick to heaven.

'Anonymous letters! What dastardly creature could –'

'Who knows? A discarded lover, another woman, a jealous companion, or, quite simply, a monster. . . . The world is full of them.'

'Then that is why you were so cold the day I got home?'

'I did not know what attitude to adopt. I kept on wondering whether this adventure of yours was serious or not, a passing fancy or a genuine passion. Neither your

173

return, nor distance, had made you forget. I knew, from Alexis, that you watched for the coming of the post. I even got him to show me one of the envelopes, with a Lima stamp, and your address written in large capitals, which was a clumsy way of not attracting attention.'

Fontane tried to defend Dolores's intelligence.

'It wasn't a question of – hm – disguising handwriting, but of being legible.'

'And how did you manage to answer, Guillaume? I have never seen *your* letters laid out for the post.'

'I take them myself to the post-office, every two days,' he said, like a child caught out in some misdemeanour.

She stopped again, trembling.

'*You* do that! *You* who never walk a step, who never go shopping! You, every two days – for a woman you scarcely know!'

'My dear, you can't say that I scarcely know her.'

'Don't think I'm ignorant. That old Saint-Astier woman told me the other day, at the Larivières, that the two of you had travelled in company. How could you behave so irresponsibly, Guillaume?'

They reached the end of the lake. A child with a scooter separated them for a moment.

'But you must not think, Pauline, that I went to Latin America in search of adventures. Just the contrary is true. I had made up my mind, after your illness, never again to indulge in those innocent friendships which seemed to cause you so much suffering. But who could have resisted that woman? Brilliant, young, beautiful, famous?'

'And you really thought that so beautiful, so young, so brilliant a woman loved you, Guillaume?'

'Why, otherwise, should she have followed me to Bogotá? I agree that it seems surprising, but I cannot deny the evidence of my own eyes.'

'My poor friend, how credulous you are! Madame de

174

Saint-Astier, though admitting that your conquest is a highly talented actress, told me, also, that she is a coquette both on and off the stage.'

'Pauline, that may be worthy of the Saint-Astier woman, it is *not* worthy of you. I may be credulous, but I know my job as a reader, and I solemnly say that only a woman – hm – in love could have written the wonderful letters I have received.'

'So, she has written you wonderful letters? How I should like to see them! Listen, Guillaume, I will consent to go on living with you only on one condition, that you tell me *everything*. What I cannot stand is being deceived, to go on seeing you hiding away behind tricks and play-acting. If I become your *confidante* I shall no longer be *betrayed*, and, perhaps, in time, I may forgive you. Tell me, what is her name?'

'Would not that be betraying *her*?'

'In what way? I can find it out tomorrow, if I wish. The Saint-Astier woman can get it from Geoffroy. Besides, I understand that there is in Paris, at this moment, a young Chilian who was the lover of your Dulcinea before ever you came on the scene.'

This piece of news came as a shock to Fontane, but he managed, with an effort, to put a good face on it.

'That is perfectly possible. Dolores never pretended that she was a virgin, nor even that she was faithful : but she did say that the three weeks she had spent with me had been –'

'The happiest of her life? Are you, at your age, so simple-minded as to be taken in by trite phrases which are as old as mankind? But you said *Dolores*, Dolores *what*?'

'Dolores García,' he admitted with a weary sigh.

By this time, they had reached their own front-door in the rue de la Ferme.

'Will you please give me her address, Guillaume? I wish to write to her.'

'Write to her?' he said, now thoroughly alarmed, as he pushed open the gate. 'What can you have to say to her?'

'Many, many things, I can assure you: that it is not very good manners to grab a married man without bothering whether one may be causing unhappiness to somebody else: that, if she really wants you, she can have you, since I shall be in no way opposed to divorce proceedings.'

For a moment or two they said no more, because Alexis had opened the door. As soon, however, as they had taken off their outdoor things, Guillaume followed Pauline to her room.

'Divorce! There can be no question of it! Never, for an instant, have I offered her that, nor made any promise of marriage. On the contrary, I have always sung your praises to her. I have told her that we are the most united couple in the world, that I could not do without you.'

'And she accepted that? Yet you tell me that she loves you!'

'She did not accept it. She said "I don't want to hear you talk of your wife".'

'So, she addresses you in the second-person singular, does she? What I have never had in twenty-five years of marriage, she got in three weeks.'

'It is merely a question of – hm – linguistic convention, my dear. Everyone uses that form of words in Spanish. I wish you to understand, Pauline, that I have never sought to make a comparison between you, to establish anything that might be called competition. You were, you are, my wife. When that trip of mine was over, I was happy in the thought of returning to you. The proof of that is that, at the moment of our parting, Dolores was prepared to spend a fortnight with me in some remote

176

hotel, but that I refused, saying that I did not wish to
delay my return. But, damn it all, no man is entirely
single-minded, and we all of us, from time to time, have
the right to a few days of dreaming.'

'Your dreams seem to have had a very solid covering of
flesh,' she said bitterly.

At this moment Alexis brought in tea with the discreet
and worried look of an old friend who understands, but
dare not interfere.

6

AFTER this confession the atmosphere at the rue de la
Ferme was, if not happier, at least more animated. Guillaume had given his wife Dolores García's address, but
even after that, whenever husband and wife were alone
together, Pauline riddled Fontane with questions.

'How did you meet her? What did you say to her?
Which first transformed a friendship into a love-affair?
When was it that she came to your room, and what reason
did she give for doing so? What happened after that?

Since his imagination was a great deal better than his
memory, he did his best to fill the blanks, but her implacable precision at once laid bare what was invention and
what was not.

'Do not lie to me, Guillaume! You say that young
Saint-Astier asked her to the dinner he gave in your
honour, before you had even so much as mentioned her
to him. I find it impossible to believe that. Why *should* he
have invited her?'

'How do I know? Am I Saint-Astier's keeper? I suppose because she had a high reputation in her native
country.'

Often, when he had shut himself away in his library for

the whole day, Pauline's terrible interrogatories did not begin until ten at night: but once they had got started she would continue with them until two or three in the morning, with the obstinacy of a maniac. She wanted to reconstitute, in every detail, each of those fatal days.

'What was this Castillo's attitude to you, Guillaume? Did he seem jealous, or, on the contrary, triumphant?'

'How can I possibly remember? I don't treasure up with pointless exactitude, as you do, all the images of the past. There are days when even *her* face escapes me.'

'Then you *do* try to recover it?'

He frequently sat there in silence, with bent head, like a criminal being importuned by an over-zealous magistrate. Then, after five or six questions had remained unanswered, he would groan:

'You are killing me, Pauline: this is Hell!'

'Is it not worse for me?'

Longing to be allowed to go to sleep, he tried, but in vain, to stem the horrible flood. If he alluded to the time:

'I am very sure', she would say, 'that you did not count the night-hours when you were with your mistress.'

'That is where you are wrong! She called me "Cinderella" because I always sent her away at midnight.'

'What did she do then? How did she manage to get back to her own room without being detected? Was she never seen coming out of yours?'

He always ended by saying, humbly: 'I don't know: I don't know!'

He slept for only a few hours each night, and awoke in the morning tired, and without the will to work. Even Lolita's letters brought him no consolation. After a wait of three weeks he was now getting them again regularly. What, he wondered uneasily, could have been the reason for her long silence? She spoke of a trip to the Andes. Had she made it alone? She was now rehearsing in one of

Castillo's plays. There were times when some phrase gave new life to his passion: 'Your verses', she wrote, 'brought a happy smile to my lips. It has taken root there, and still remains.'

He wrote, on the day after the fatal explanation beside the lake, to give her an account of what had happened, and to warn her that she would be getting a letter from Pauline. But he could scarcely expect an answer for two weeks, and had no idea what her reaction would be. He feared that she might be so annoyed that she would at once put an end to a liaison which had no possible future. All the same, he felt that he had been 'loyal', because in this letter he had been eloquent in praise of Pauline, and had said that any violence of language in her must be forgiven in view of her present state of mind.

The only woman in Paris to whom he could speak freely about the crisis which was turning his whole life upside down, was Edmée Larivière. She had given him to understand that she knew everything, and that, though she could not condone his behaviour, she was perfectly prepared to let him confide in her. He paid her long visits which were a source of the most lively pleasure to him, because it is always agreeable to talk of what one loves, and more agreeable still to talk of it to a sympathetic woman. He thought that his romantic adventure had given him an added lustre in Edmée's eyes, and it was certainly true that it was she who sought these meetings. When the substance of love is absent, women delight in the smell, the echo, the reflection of it.

'I know', he said, 'that I should grant Pauline a plenary indulgence, because I stand in very great need of the same from her: all the same, there are limits to what a man can stand. This daily and nightly reconstruction of the crime! Why on earth does she make me tell her ten, twenty times over things which can be only painful to her, and about which, my memory being uncertain, I contradict myself more and more?'

Edmée assumed her angelic doctor expression.

'We women', she said, 'love dotting the i's and crossing the t's, Guillaume. We never get tired of analysing a situation or of dissecting a feeling. You men live a life of action – even the novelists, because, to them, the writing of a book is action. We are ready to dwell on happiness and unhappiness for long periods. I do so understand Pauline.'

'I, alas! must confess that I have long ceased to understand her. What does she want? Sometimes she gives me my freedom and writes long epistles to Dolores in which, I imagine, abuse alternates with generosity. Sometimes she says that my happiness is her happiness, that she will put no obstacles in the way of our meeting again, that all she asks is that she shall not be lied to, that she shall be treated as a trusted friend. If I can believe what she tells me, she has written to Dolores saying: "Do you want my husband? He is all yours. You are younger and more beautiful than I am. I will gracefully bow myself out. Come, carry him off and marry him." The unfortunate Lolita must have been knocked sideways. She has never suggested such a thing. It would be wonderful for me to see her again, and I can envisage with pleasure a rendez-vous in Seville, Granada, or some paradise in the Andes. But of Dolores in Paris! of divorce and re-marriage, there can be no question!'

'Fortunately,' said Edmée, 'I can't see you, Guillaume dear, married to an actress, perpetually jealous, haunting the back stage of provincial theatres! Besides, there is Pauline to be thought of. You mustn't let yourself be taken in by all this renunciation business: that's all just put on. Pauline might give you up to somebody else from pride, but she would die of it. I met her yesterday at the

Ménétriers, and I tell you, she is quite literally devastated by suffering. Never forget, Guillaume, that your wife's love for you is something very wonderful. From the first moment she met you, no other man has meant anything to her, and that, God knows! is rare.'

'Ah!' he said: 'I feel torn in pieces! One thing, though, is certain, we can't go on like this: what's to be done?'

'Be tougher with her,' said Edmée. 'Women shouldn't be given their heads: they need governing.'

After Fontane had left, Claire Ménétrier, who, no less than Edmée, was curious about the business, happened to look in.

'Pauline', said Claire, 'is like a lioness deprived of her young. She is looking for the truth with wild and haggard eyes. She has started off on the hunt with passionate indiscretion, hoping to find out something about her rival. Would you believe it, she has actually been to tea with Wanda? She has, indeed, my dear, because she wanted to meet the young Chilian who was once Dolores García's lover.'

'So you know the lady's name,' said Edmée.

'Certainly I do. I, too, wanted to make the Chilian's acquaintance. He is charming, and was wildly in love with the woman.'

'So all that Guillaume says of her must be true. Why did the Chilian let her go?'

'One need have only five minutes' talk with him to realize that he didn't. But he knows that any lasting happiness with her would be impossible, at least for him. He's certainly a very personable young man.'

'How does he explain this liaison with Guillaume?'

'What he says is shrewd and probably true. According to him she is, first and foremost, an actress, and looks on each love affair as an opportunity to play a new role, in which it is her ambition to give a perfect performance. In this she succeeds, and, so long as she is on the stage, has complete belief in the character she is interpreting. With Fontane she decided to be the young companion of an elderly writer, at once an admirer and a lover. She built up the part to perfection, and was quite adorable in it. So, you see, the impression Guillaume got was accurate enough. This young Santo-Quevedo is, however, of the opinion that, since Guillaume left, she may have met some-one else, and be playing, for his benefit, quite a different part though just as perfectly.'

'I see,' said Edmée. 'But she doesn't seem to have forgot-ten Guillaume quite so quickly as that view argues. He read to me, only a few days ago, several highly emotional and really delightful letters he had had from her.'

'Why not? She is now playing the part of a woman who writes highly emotional and delightful letters to her distant lover.'

'Poor Pauline! It is no easy thing for us wretched bread-and-butter wives to put up an efficient defence against actresses! They have talent, technique, and prestige. And then, you know, art always seems to be truer than nature.'

'Are we not all of us actresses?' said Claire.

'That is true, but we haven't, all of us, got talent. Still, I think that Pauline will win in the long run, unless, that is, she spoils her game by being too violent. Just at present, Guillaume is contrite: remorse has made him indulgent. But I can see that his nerves are all on edge as a result of the same old scene, sometimes unspoken, sometimes spoken only too loudly, which his wife stages every night. We must never forget that Dolores García is essentially an actress, Guillaume essentially a writer: and a writer who can no longer write, is apt to go mad.'

'Men', said Claire, rising to go, 'are victimized by pas-sions. They don't love them.'

7

GUILLAUME FONTAINE understood less and less the actions and reactions of his wife and his mistress. Pauline was now writing almost every day to Dolores, was even sending her presents – a piece of jewellery, a printed silk scarf. 'Ought I to thank her?' wrote Dolores to Guillaume. 'As a result of what you told me, I have always had feelings of respect and admiration for your wife. I hate to think that I am the cause of someone's sufferings.' Nevertheless, she continued her letter in terms that were 'tiernas y enamoradas'. She wasn't, it was clear, trying to bring about a rupture. He advised her to thank his wife and, at the beginning of March, Pauline let her husband see, with a sort of pride, that an envelope with the Lima stamp, and the bold capitals, had arrived, addressed, this time, to *Madame* Guillaume Fontane. That evening she spoke again, until a late hour, of surrendering Guillaume to the 'Occitanian'. It was thus, remembering the last loves of Chateaubriand, that she referred, quite inaccurately, to Dolores. Tired of the whole business, completely worn out and shattered, he began to feel that one fine day he would be in the position of a disillusioned, and only too clear-sighted Sancho Panza between these two Ladies Errant.

One morning, Alexis announced mysteriously that a 'foreign gentleman' was insisting on 'seeing monsieur'.

'I took the liberty, sir, of disturbing you because the gentleman is the same gentleman who arranged your journey, sir, last summer. I thought –'

'You were perfectly right, Alexis – show the gentleman

in. .... Ovidius! how are you, my dear friend, and where have you sprung from? I last saw you at Bogotá, that place of delight and damnation. What have you been doing since then?'

'Master, I did stay on for a little at Bogotá, then I covered your route in the reversed direction: Lima, Santiago, Buenos Aires, Montevideo, for to organize a tour. Then I paid a visit to my New York office. From there I have been in Italy, Greece, Egypt. Do you know Egypt, master? It is a country where you are adored. It is enough to say "Guillaume Fontane" and all the Egyptians they turn up their eyes. That is not a flattery, but the truth, and nothing more. I am going to make a tour for you, master: Alexandria, the Cairo and back by Athens, Roma! It will be a triumph!'

'No, no, my friend. In spite of your energy, which is truly terrifying, and your eloquence which is quite – hm – Ciceronian, you won't get me on the road again. In the first place, it is very doubtful whether I could leave Paris. I have been working badly this winter, and my poor wife is far from well. If ever I let myself be tempted, it would rather be by a request to go back to the continent which you revealed to me, and of which I have retained such – hm – paradisiacal memories. Yes, if you offered me *that* chance, I would gladly return, not tomorrow, but at some more distant date, to Peru, Colombia –'

Petresco made a gesture of impatience.

'Master, even though you are muchly loved in those countries, you cannot go there every year. The public, it wants new names and new faces. Maybe, in two, three years – and I would like more Argentina and Brazil than Peru and Colombia where the public who understand French it is small, small. .... I have lost there much money ...'

Fontane's expression was one of confidential modesty.

184

'If I have Peru in mind, dear friend, that is because I have been conducting a correspondence with the charming lady to whom you introduced me at Lima: Dolores García. She writes very delightful letters.'

Petresco who, as a rule, was deferential even to excess, replied abruptly:

'How? that still lasts? Ah! master, master!' Then he asked whether he might present his respects to Madame Fontane. Fontane, foreseeing the torrent of questions which would descend upon Ovidius, said:

'No, my friend, I think you had really better not. As I told you, my wife is far from well, and is seeing nobody.'

Petresco became indulgent, and a shade annoyed:

'I regret it, master, I regret it enormously, because I have a great sympathy with Madame Fontane!'

'It almost seems as though he is reading me a lesson,' thought Guillaume, and put a rather unceremonious end to the interview.

Somewhat later, Pauline Fontane was called to the telephone to Ovid Petresco. He began to explain who he was but she stopped him.

'I have not forgotten you, monsieur. What is it you want?'

He said that he very much wanted to speak to her, quite alone, without 'the master Fontane' knowing anything about it.

'I excuse myself for insisting, Madame Fontane, but this, it is enormously important, not for me, but for the master and for you. I can preserve you from a great danger.'

Pauline was far too curious about everything that had to do with what she called 'that fatal journey', not to be tempted. The only objection she made was that, at the rue de la Ferme, all visitors ran a considerable risk of running into her husband.

'In that case,' said Petresco, 'we must meet ourselves in town. That is easy. There is a small bar where I often go in the rue Tronchet, and there you would surely not meet with anyone you know, especially in the morning. Would it be all right tomorrow at eleven o'clock?'

After a moment's hesitation, she agreed.

On the following day she stopped her car at the Printemps, made her way through the shop, and looked about for the little bar, the name of which Petresco had given her. She was excited, worried, intrigued, and ill at ease. She had never in her life agreed to a secret meeting with anybody, and dreaded in advance what this man, whose name was linked with the worst misfortune of her life, might have to say to her. But with the determination and the self-assurance of the true maniac, she entered, with quiet deliberation, the dark, narrow interior, down the whole length of which wooden tables and benches were arranged on either side, each table being separated from its neighbours by a partition. The first of these was occupied by two youngsters who were handling and swapping postage-stamps, and writing down figures on two sheets of paper. A few paces farther on, she caught sight of Petresco, who had risen to his feet. He came towards her, kissed her hand, sat down at an isolated table, and asked what she would like to drink:

'Nothing, thank you. I am not accustomed to drinking, especially not at this time of day.'

'But I shall have to order something: a fruit-juice, yes? Waiter, one orange-juice and one porto flip.'

Then he assumed his pained and serious look.

'Madame Fontane, I have wished to see you because I have thought it is my duty to put you on your guard. As I have said on the telephone, I have enormously respect and sympathy for you, and for the master, admirations and affections. For these reasons I do not wish it that the dignity of your home shall be compromised. Ah! Madame Fontane, how you were wrong not to hear me when I begged you to accompany your husband! You do not know what it is – a man alone in a country where the women, they are bewitching!'

Two men sat down at the table opposite. They looked as though they had been made up as gangsters. They were talking together in low voices, and, from time to time, Pauline caught a few words: 'Three units – get rid of King.' She felt as though she were involved in a bad film. When she spoke it was with considerable difficulty.

'If it is of Dolores García that you wish to talk to me, let me say at once that I am already informed. My husband has told me everything, and I, myself, have been in communication with the person in question. On one point, however, which concerns me nearly, you can be informative. How did their liaison begin? Which of them took the first step, she or he?'

'She! After the first evening, she say to me: "Petresco, I shall have that man!" Madame Fontane, you did not listen to me one time, I warn you, and I say, Take care, Now, for a second time, I warn you, and I say, Take care, Madame Fontane. Dolores is not a woman of whom one forgets when she does not wish it.'

'She is very beautiful?'

'More than beautiful! She is a fairy, an enchantress!'

'And why should she wish to see my husband again? A fairy can raise up other lovers with a touch of her wand.'

'Why? Madame Fontane, with women, who can ever say why? Of the master, she expects that he shall bring her to Paris, that he write plays for her. I say to you: "Madame Fontane, do not let her come here, or you are lost!" The master, he loves you. When he talks of you

187

there are no too beautiful words. Only, he has almost sixty years.'

'And she is, I know, twenty-five,' said Pauline.

'No, madame, she has thirty ! I have seen her passport. But the charm, it is beyond describing. As soon as she sees the master, she will take him back. Believe me. I am your ally, first, because I esteem you, and also because I wish to take the master into other countries – Egypt – Italy. But there you shall be with us, Madame Fontane. ... You must : without that it will begin all over again. Another orange-juice?'

She stayed a little while longer, harrying him with direct and detailed questions. In matters of dates, times, and facts he was no less vague than Guillaume. When she realized that she could get no more out of him, she left.

On the Place de la Madeleine there were several flower-stalls. She bought some chrysanthemums : 'mourning flowers', she thought. 'From now on, those are the appropriate wear for me.'

8

PASSIONATE love is an ailment with a well-recognized graph of rise and fall. But, just as a skilled and experienced doctor, when attacked by a cancer of the ordinary type, does not recognize in himself what, if he found it in others, would leave no doubt in his mind about the true diagnosis, so did Fontane now enter on a period of convalescence, though he did not realize that he was doing so. The letters which he exchanged with Dolores were still 'loving and tender', but the rhythm of the correspondence was becoming slower. On the other hand, between Dolores and Pauline it was accelerating. Guillaume had no idea what the two women were saying to one another, but feared that they might be entering into some strange alliance against him.

Fontane's friends who had been, some of them alarmed, others secretly pleased, at the time of his return when the first rolling of thunder had made itself heard, were astonished to see the storm receding with so little noise. Edmée Larivière invited Guillaume to take tea with her alone.

'What is the matter, Guillaume dear?' she asked him. 'I have been thinking for some time now that you were looking melancholy. You came back from your tour a young and ardent conquistador; but now the warmth seems to have abated. What is the news of your sentimental troubles?'

'My sentimental troubles, as you call them, are at slack water. How could it be otherwise? They have, for nourishment, nothing but a thin crop of memories. After six months all that could be said about the past, has been said. You will tell me that there is still the present. That, no doubt, is true, but our presents are distinct, different, remote from one another. For us both, art is the main motive of our lives. Dolores tells me about the plays she is rehearsing – O'Neill's *Mourning Becomes Electra*; *Partage de midi*, which she is still waiting for the author's permission to produce; an *auto sacramental* and *Le Fils prodigue*, which I don't know. I read with a not very attentive eye, and tell her in return about the novel I want to write. It can't be of much interest to the poor child, for she makes no reference to it in her answers. She knows nothing of the people I see; I know nothing of those by whom she is surrounded. What is there left? The future? For a long time I wrote to her hopefully about our meetings to be: "When are you coming to Granada, to Seville?" I used to ask her: "When shall we return together to Medellín?" I still long for those meetings, but have almost given up hope that they will materialize. There is one thing I must say, which I think will surprise you : if Pauline had not entered this circuit and increased its power, the current would already have ceased to flow.'

'How sad, Guillaume! It seemed to be such a really great love.'

'Even the greatest love needs nourishment.'

'Does Pauline still correspond with her? That seems so odd to me. What *can* they have to say to each other?'

'They neither of them confide in me. My own impression is that sometimes they abuse one another like Homer's goddesses, and sometimes carry on a warm and mutual friendship, at my expense.'

'Why *at your expense?*'

'Because women always stand by one another: you should know that better than I do.'

'It is all a great deal more complex,' said Edmée broodingly. '*Rivalry* is a more usual thing between women, rivalry for the possession of the man they both love, but once the two women have agreed, no matter how temporarily, on a *modus vivendi* in their relations with him, then, a harem takes shape, and they, both of them, try to forget their slavery in abusing the Sultan. In this case, Pauline is prepared neither to surrender nor to share her master. But, tell me, Guillaume, why do you not put up a more effective defence of a love which, as you have so often told me, brought you such wonderful happiness? That "rejuvenation", that "increase of vitality", as you put it, was important. Are you prepared to surrender it?'

'There would be no need for me to give it up if only Pauline would make an effort to understand that I sometimes feel the need of gaiety, of caprice, of tenderness, and would make an effort to provide them. She could, you know. Pauline is very much a woman. She has many gifts, but she seems to have made it a point of honour now to remain bogged down in a purely negative attitude.

Between these two Castilians, I am, as it were – hm – at a loss.'

For a few moments Edmée said nothing; then:

'In my opinion, the important thing is to find out what *you* want. You can change neither Pauline nor your Périchole, and you can't keep both of them indefinitely. You have got to *choose*. The longer I live, my dear Guillaume, the more convinced do I become that the whole of wisdom lies in that one word. Take my own case. I was quite pretty . . .'

'You were beautiful, very beautiful, and still are.'

'However that may be, I was pretty enough to please. I had the offer of endless adventures. Do you think I wasn't tempted? But the fact remains that, married twice, I have been twice faithful. I made my choice.'

'What I need', said Fontane, 'is to be completely alone for a bit, so as to have a chance of getting to terms with myself.'

9

THE 'solitude cure' which Fontane made in Lorraine, was effective. The house, left to Pauline by Boersch, stood on the highest point of a gentle rise. From its windows he could see the Moselle with its fringe of willows, alders, and poplars, and the priest's kitchen-garden which Pauline, herself, had brought into existence. The marvellous silence was broken only by the twittering of birds which nested in a great beech, the branches of which swayed gently to and fro close to the stone balcony. He worked all morning, rejoicing in the tranquillity of the early hours, and, after luncheon, took a walk along the narrow path which skirted the river. The animal and vegetable life around him gave rise to feelings of humility.

'All the same,' he said to himself, 'the fact that willows and swallows grow old as men grow old, does not really cure the pain I feel at the coming of old age.'

Then, feeling alert, lithe, and intellectually rich with huge projects: 'Is old age my trouble? No, but the bad use I make of it. A *prayer for the right employment of old age:* "I praise Thee, O Lord, and I will bless Thee all my life long, for having gently loosed, one after the other, all those bonds of the flesh which made me cling to illusory hopes."' He stopped on a little beach of white sand washed by the rippling water. The purity of the air was a delight, and he drew in deep gulps of it. 'Old age', he thought, 'is not decay but deliverance. Life should return without a struggle to that nature from which it comes. If individuality is slowly thinned away, communion with the world becomes possible.' Several times he repeated: 'Joyful Acceptance.'

White coils of flimsy mist rose from the valley. Never had this chaste and virile countryside seemed to him more beautiful. 'No,' he said to himself, 'not in littleness should one end. Again I ask, is it old age that has been my trouble? All I really suffered from was, as Edmée said, my refusal to make an act of choice. But that refusal was, really, pure illusion. In point of fact, I had chosen. Twice I have seen Pauline sicken, and twice I could not endure the sight. There was nothing to stop me from sacrificing her, yet I did not do so. Tomorrow, in similar circumstances, I should act in the same way. I have reached what, a year ago, would have seemed to me a trite conclusion, that in love the gratification of the senses counts for almost nothing. Its pleasures are delightful and sharp, but they do not suffice to create a durable bond. A healthy man regards them with cynicism, and he is right. True love is a craving for the sublime. It was that I have been seeking in Pauline and Dolores. I looked for it in Dolores because

Pauline has disappointed, after having for a long time fulfilled me.'

He stopped to look at a spot of red which seemed to be dancing. What was it? Forest fire, or the setting sun reflected back from a window? He continued with his walk. 'No, it is not true that I turned to Dolores out of spite. I turned to her because she wanted me, and because she is irresistible. Because I had to have some reason for admiring her, I fitted her with a personality cut to *my* measure. I imagined her to have the gift of constancy, and to be entirely concerned with me. That was not so, nor ever could have been. Dolores was not to blame. She never gave me any promise that she would surrender her liberty for my sake. And all the time I never realized that I had, close beside me, the great spirit for which I had been looking. For Pauline, with all her faults, has got that purity, that gift of total fidelity, which I had sought in vain in a chameleon temperament.'

Several fine cows were walking towards him across the meadow. 'The sort of fidelity which I demanded, but was not prepared, myself, to give. Fidelity is not natural in the male. But nothing really beautiful ever is natural. Man's greatness lies in the fact that he can commit himself, even if it means death. These cows have no painful duties, no torments of conscience, but, then, they are cows!'

When he got back to the house, the post had come. There was a letter from Lolita. For a long while he looked at the handsome capitals, which had so often set his heart thumping, then opened the envelope. Dolores described a festival at Lima in which she had scored a personal triumph in a play by Pedro-Maria Castillo:

'I wore a white dress, off the shoulders. You would have been mad about it. When I made my first entrance, I thought of you, just to bolster up my self-confidence.

Does that please you, *no*? I am vexed to think that you have never seen me on the stage. Do you know what I want more than anything in the world? To play in a Paris theatre, first in Spanish, so as to get myself known, then in French. If you could arrange that, I would come at once. . . . '

He re-read the letter several times, trying to understand the full meaning of what she was saying. Did she really think of him except when she was writing?

That evening, when he was alone in his room, he sat down to answer her.

GUILLAUME FONTANE *to* DOLORES GARCÍA

I feel sad at not having been one of the spectators at your triumph, *querida*, but no doubt it was better so. You must, that evening, have been surrounded, praised, and courted. I should have revelled in my admiration, and suffered because of your admirers. So, you have become my wife's friend! You exchange the most mysterious letters. This has created between us an odd and rather disquieting atmosphere. I accept my destiny, but not without regrets.

I owe to you the loveliest days of my dwindling years. Shall I ever know again that sense of a flaming brightness? I do not think so. You had, you have, a great deal of charm, Lolita, and you would not be easy to replace. I shall make no attempt to replace you. I shall keep the memory. It will do something to give fragrance to a happy, but somewhat grey, existence, as an armful of wild flowers, plucked in the fields, brings light into a work-room. That is how I feel this evening, while the moon is rising behind the poplars, and the owl comes out from his tower. What will happen, and what will become of these wise thoughts if, tomorrow, you turn up in

Paris? I think that your coming would create a difficult situation, sometimes painful, often delicious. *Ne nos inducas in tentationem.* I am here for three months. I dream of the olive grove, of the church bells of Bogotá, of the Cali plane. It needs very little to keep an old heart alive.

This letter gives a pretty exact idea of Fontane's state of mind at that time. He was like a sleeper suddenly awakened, who sees clearly the real objects around him, but still wonders at the scraps of dreams which float in his mind and slowly dissipate, like the morning mist.

Throughout the whole of that summer which, for him, was a time of hard work, and peace of mind, his determination to rebuild his domestic existence grew stronger. Often, as he looked from his window at the dead water of the canal and the sparkling river, he meditated upon the charm of the romantic, and decided that it should be sought rather in the deepening of a stable love than in ephemeral affairs.

'Only that which is not known can arouse the craving to know? ... True enough. But is there not a great deal that is unknown in every human being?' ...

Of this truth, each day brought him further proof. Pauline had joined him, and he found it more difficult than ever to understand her attitude. She scarcely even mentioned Dolores, and discussed intelligently with Guillaume the book on which he was at work. He complained about her being so distant.

'What do you expect?' she said. 'Confidence once lost is not easy to re-establish. I am still wholly devoted to you, but I cannot forget that you have done something of which I thought you incapable. That face and that body will always be between you and me.'

'But what if the effect of that mistake has been to

195

strengthen my attachment to you, has led me to understand, and to feel that, for me, you are irreplaceable?'

'I, Guillaume, had no need of equatorial adventure to reveal that knowledge and that feeling.'

He thought that she was being unjust, that she was stuck fast in her resentment, at a time when he was making a great effort to draw closer to her. But he was patient. When the anniversary of his first meeting with Dolores approached, Pauline once more showed signs of nervousness. She had an inborn superstition about dates. A letter from Lolita informed Guillaume that she was going to play *Tessa* again: 'Does it not please you to think of me as the "Constant Nymph"?' Next day, he replied with a letter which he meant her to understand as a farewell.

GUILLAUME FONTANE *to* DOLORES GARCÍA

Yes, certainly it pleases me to think that my own nymph is, in her own way, constant. I, no more than you, forget our enchanted hours. It is almost a year now, Lolita, since we first met. When the anniversary of that day comes round, go, if you are in Lima, to the little baroque church of La Magdalena, and think of me for a moment. No one can give her life to one who is for ever absent, but she *can* give him a moment – and a prayer. Was it all real? There are times, in this quiet countryside, when I find it hard to believe. Then my memories drift up from the depths: your first look, which made me your slave; your long-fingered hand pushing up your curls; your face transfigured by ardour or by penitence. These images have remained so clear in my mind, that the ineffaceable dream causes me neither remorse nor repentance. It is like some very beautiful book I might have read, which has told, as the result of some miraculous divination on the part of the author, the story of the life I wanted to live. Who knows? Perhaps it is better that, having emerged one evening against the background of a mysterious city belonging to a magical and unreal world, you should again withdraw without having lost anything of your supernatural grace. You will always be for me the woman who can never grow old, and never change. As for me, alas! how much to my interest it is that I should exist for you only in the world of memory, the only world in which my last days of youth can be preserved from the darkness which now lies so close ahead of me. Adieu.

That evening, he said to Pauline:

'Today, I wrote my last letter to Dolores.'

'Your last?'

'Yes. I hope so. That page is turned. On the next one, which is still blank, I want only you to write.'

'But don't you know, Guillaume, that Dolores is coming to Paris in November?'

He was completely bowled over by this news:

'What! She had vaguely mentioned such a possibility, but had never said it was a certainty, still less, so imminent. . . . Are you sure?'

'Quite sure. She and I have arranged the whole thing together. In October, she is to make a tour in Spain, after which she, and her Compagnie des Andes, as it is called, will give a few performances in Paris. I have myself negotiated, on their behalf, with the Comédie des Champs-Élysées.'

'You! What an act of madness, Pauline! Why did you do it?'

'Out of curiosity, and, perhaps, to put you to the test, Guillaume.'

'Dolores can play only in Spanish. No one will go to see her.'

'Oh yes, they will. We need only create a snob interest.

Now, at last, you will see your actress exercising her art.'

Guillaume had become very gloomy. After a long silence, he said:

'If Dolores really comes to Paris, I shall make arrangements to be elsewhere.'

Pauline sat with downcast eyes, saying nothing.

10

UNTIL the days immediately preceding the arrival of Dolores García in Paris, Pauline Fontane had not believed that her husband would have the courage to go away. She had made Dolores promise that, should she see Guillaume again, she would not try to re-assert her power over him, and Dolores had given her word. Fontane's determined attitude, therefore, seemed now rather pointless. When he heard from his wife that Lolita would be landing at Santander early in November, he accepted an invitation to lecture in Switzerland during the whole of that month. It was his version of having himself tied to the mast while the Sirens sang. By the time Dolores and her company reached Paris, he was in Zürich.

From Spain, where she had been playing for the past fortnight, Dolores had written several letters to Pauline, some of them enthusiastic, others querulous. She was filled with excitement at visiting a country to which her heart owed so great a debt, and Granada, Seville, and Toledo had come up to her most exaggerated expectations, though she had to admit that the reception accorded to her company had been disappointing. The attitude of the Spanish critics to 'this group of players with a provincial accent' had been one of contemptuous indulgence. A few connoisseurs had praised the acting of

Dolores García, and one great writer, Ramón de Martina, had followed the company from place to place with passionate perseverance. Dolores enclosed a photograph of herself sitting at the feet of the old poet who was shown gazing sentimentally into her eyes. The financial results, however, had been poor, and the actress, saddened and discouraged, had now focused all her hopes on Paris. 'If Paris likes us, nothing else will matter,' she wrote to Madame Fontane, adding that she would be at the Hôtel Montalembert on the fifth, and that the season would open on the ninth.

The two women had arranged to meet at the hotel about six o'clock. Pauline, in a state of extreme emotional nervousness, was careful to choose the dress and the hat which, according to Guillaume, most became her. When she arrived, she said to the Reception Clerk:

'Madame Dolores García?'

He spoke into the house-telephone:

'Room 218? Madame Fontane is downstairs.'

Then, to that lady, he said:

'Madame García will be with you in a moment.'

Pauline sat down in an armchair facing the lift, and waited for the face with which so many photographs had made her familiar. Very soon, the lift appeared, and she made as though to rise, but the only person who emerged from it was a fat man with fair hair. At that moment, Pauline, raising her eyes as though under the influence of a magnetic attraction, saw on the stairs a very beautiful young woman with a slim waist and a long cigarette-holder in one corner of her mouth, standing on one of the treads and looking at her. She recognized Dolores, who came down very slowly with her eyes still fixed on her.

'What a genius for production!' thought Madame Fontane. Only when Dolores was close to her did she notice the red-gold hair, the sea-green eyes, and that

199

perfect carriage which combined reserve with affectionate gravity. She got up.

'So this is you!' murmured Dolores in a voice eloquent of restrained emotion.

'What perfect inflexion!' thought Pauline again, in spite of herself. 'Without any undue emphasis she has established the importance of this meeting: not at all Rachel playing Racine.'

She suddenly realized the full extent of Guillaume's sacrifice.

'I should have recognized you anywhere,' said Dolores. 'You are exactly as I expected you to be, beautiful and pure.'

'You, too,' said Pauline, 'are precisely as I thought you would be: beautiful and dangerous.'

Dolores sat down; her smile was frank and easy.

'Dangerous? Not for you. I shall keep my promise – you believe me, *no*?'

'I believe you the more, since it will be easy for you to do so,' said Pauline on a note of modest triumph. 'My husband has left Paris, and will not be back again during your visit. But we will speak of him later. Today, I want only to offer you my services as guide to the places you would like to see, as a possible useful companion to you in your shopping, and as someone who can provide introductions to people who may be of use to you. ... Would you like me to arrange a lunch-party? I hope that all goes well at the theatre?'

The receptionist approached:

'Madame García is wanted on the telephone.'

While Pauline waited for her to come back, she reflected: 'Guillaume did not lie: her charm is irresistible. Am I already under her thumb?'

Dolores reappeared:

'I must ask you to forgive me,' she said; 'that was the

secretary-general of the theatre. He insists on my dining with him tonight. He is nice, and is helping us a great deal.'

'You mean young Nerciat? Yes, he is very nice,' said Pauline. 'When are you opening?'

'On Thursday night, with *Bodas de sangre*. We shall have our dress-reheasal on Wednesday. Until then I am free. Won't you have a Porto? or a cocktail? No? Do you mind if I order a Martini?'

She summoned a passing waiter, gave him her order, and then said, in a tone which sounded part tender and part shy :

'You are being very sweet to me, and very much the great lady. Yes, I shall like very much to have luncheon with you, and to do my sight-seeing in Paris in your company, *Pauline* – you do not mind if I call you Pauline? – "Madame" makes me feel awkward : I know you so well, and for me it would be a pleasure if you would call me *Dolores*. It will be a proof that you have forgiven me just a little bit. I never wished to do you any harm, you know that, *no*?'

A caressing note, a note of supplication, had come into her voice. Pauline said that the hall of the hotel was hardly the place for explanations, and that they would resume their conversation later. For the moment, all they need do was fix a time and a place for a meeting next morning.

'Where do you want to go? Notre-Dame? Saint-Séverin? the Louvre?'

'Oh, yes, all those, but also the rue de la Paix and the Tomb of Napoleon. But above all, I want to go to a theatre.'

'Would you care to come with me, the day after to-morrow, to the Comédie-Française? They are playing *Le Chandelier*.'

'Ah!' said Lolita, as though happiness were giving her a heart-attack. 'Of that I have been dreaming for years!'

She emptied her Martini at a gulp, lit another cigarette, and added:

'Here, in the hotel, I have with me two girl friends, two companions, Conchita and Corinna. Would it be possible for me to bring them, too? It would make them so happy.'

'Nothing easier,' said Pauline with an air of authority. 'I have only to ask the administrator for a box.'

She found a certain pleasure in making it clear that, in Paris, she could exercise her power. The two women talked on for some time, and completed their plans for the next day. Dolores was again called to the telephone, and said, when she came back:

'That was our ambassador. He has asked me to take "pot-luck" with them this evening.'

'How well you speak French!'

'That is because of Sister Agnes. I owe much to her.'

Pauline got up:

'Is there nothing', she asked, 'that I can do for you between now and tomorrow?'

'No. Ah! yes, there is – I should like to ask you for the address of a confessor, and also for that of your hairdresser.'

Pauline could not keep from smiling. On her way out, she thought: 'How quaint and seductive she is! Guillaume has shown a considerable amount of courage in refusing to meet her.'

She was amazed to find how little she had suffered during the conversation.

'How simple it all is,' she said to herself, 'once one has taken the plunge.'

II

NEXT day, after luncheon, Pauline drove to the Hôtel Montalembert, and sent up her name. A few minutes later, three pretty girls came down, prattling away in Spanish. Dolores introduced her two friends. Conchita was a dark-haired Andalusian with waved hair. Corinna, who was smaller, had the immense eyes and the tiny feet of a Peruvian. Both spoke French, though less well than Dolores.

Pauline retained a sunny memory of the day. The three girls' admiration of all they saw in Paris, their birdlike twittering, their unintelligible and rapid chirps, all seemed to her to be charming and exotic. The weather was fine, and the city's monuments stood out clearly against a cloudless sky. Pauline felt proud of Paris, and pleased to be able to do the honours to these enthusiastic foreigners. Notre-Dame overwhelmed them. Dolores spoke of Quasimodo and Esmeralda, then, as soon as she was inside the cathedral, fell to her knees on the stone paving. She prayed for some time, beating her breast.

'I should like also to pray in the chapels,' she said solemnly.

In front of each altar she kneeled, remained for some time with her face hidden in her hands, and then got to her feet with a look of ecstasy. She insisted on touching with her keys a shrine which contained relics.

'It is *necessary*,' she said to Pauline. 'You must do it, too.'

'But why?'

'So that your keys may open only on to happiness.'

On their way out, she noticed a pretty child being led

by its mother, pounced on it, and took it in her arms.

'What a love!' she said. 'I cannot see a *niño* without embracing it.'

She passed it on to Conchita and to Corinna, both of whom fondled it. The child seemed to be fascinated, the mother terrified.

In the car, Dolores started to hum one of her *flamenco* songs in a throaty voice. Her companions joined in. She had passed her arm through that of Pauline, who felt as though she were being gradually enveloped in an atmosphere of youth and irresponsibility in which all reserve melted away. In the rue Bonaparte and the rue des Saints-Pères, Lolita wanted to get out and walk, to go into the bookshops and buy books on the theatre, the ballet, and modern painters.

'But my dear child,' said Pauline, 'you will have a packing-case full of them!'

'The holds of the ships are large,' said Dolores.

At the Invalides, she flung herself violently to her knees in front of the balustrade which surrounds the Tomb of Napoleon. They could hear her murmured prayers.

'I have prayed for the repose of his soul,' she said. 'He is my hero.'

Conchita, who had vague memories of Joseph Bonaparte, made some objections in Spanish. All three embarked upon a heated discussion of the Emperor. The vaults of the Invalides sent back the echo of their chirrupings. About five o'clock, when it was beginning to get dark, Madame Fontane suggested that they should have tea in a *pâtisserie*, but they insisted on her going back with them to their hotel.

'We will order tea for you,' said Dolores, 'and cocktails for ourselves.'

She made Pauline go upstairs to see their rooms. On a table stood an enormous candle.

'We brought it from Peru,' explained Corinna. 'It has been blessed. It is for the storms and the tempests. When the thunder comes, you light it, say a decade of the rosary, and then you are protected against the lightning.'

Pauline found it difficult to leave them. Not for years had she spent so entertaining a day.

Next morning, at half past twelve, she sent the car for Dolores. She had improvised a luncheon-party at the rue de la Ferme. She was expecting a famous actor, Léon Laurent, Jenny, the woman novelist, the Bertrand Schmitts, the Christian Ménétriers, young Hervé Marcenat, who had recently made his bow as a dramatic critic, and Claude Nerciat, the Secretary-General of the Comédie des Champs-Élysées. Dolores, who had no sense of time, and, in any case, thought it barbarous to lunch so early, was late. The others, to whom Pauline had explained that the occasion was to be in honour of a Peruvian actress, were awaiting her arrival with the liveliest curiosity. Though rumours of scandal are as quickly forgotten, in Paris, as they are originated, the women, clearly, the men, more confusedly, remembered that there had been some sort of a drama in the Fontane *ménage*, of which an actress had been the central figure.

'Is it the same woman?' Isabelle Schmitt asked Claire Ménétrier. 'I must say, I think it highly unlikely. Guillaume is out of Paris, and Pauline, at least, the Pauline *we* know, is not the type of woman to invite her husband's mistress.'

'You can never be quite sure with Pauline; there's a largish streak of subtlety in her. . . . What is the woman's name – Dolores García? I seem to remember that *was* the person all the tittle-tattle was about.'

'Then, how about Guillaume?'

'He's gone to earth, and left the two Amazons to fight it out.'

'But they don't seem at all anxious to do any fighting!'

Dolores had her usual success. The consensus of opinion was that she was beautiful, spoke French wonderfully well, and had a most charming way with her. To each of the men she said exactly what was most likely to gratify him: to Léon Laurent, that she had tremendously enjoyed his playing at Buenos Aires; to Bertrand Schmitt, that she always read his novels, and loved them; to Ménétrier, that her greatest ambition was to act *Viviane*.

'She's got exactly the right build for the part,' said Laurent, who was studying her with great attention.

At luncheon, the conversation moved easily. Laurent talked, in his jerky manner, about the actor's craft, insisting that no one should risk his chances in the profession unless he had a true vocation, that is to say, the ability and the desire to get under the skin of a character.

'What always strikes me,' said Ménétrier, 'is the rapidity with which the player can change his, or her, whole personality. I talk with an actress in the wings. She is absorbed by domestic problems, by some theatre quarrel, or is interested, to the exclusion of everything else, in a fur coat. But the moment she steps on to the stage, she is all tears. It is more extraordinary still on a film-set, for there the performer has to repeat, again and again, the same scrap of a "shot", and each time, he, or she, produces precisely the correct intonation.'

'That is no more surprising', said Léon Laurent, 'than the singer's ability always to hit the right note at the right moment. Once an inflection has been captured and registered, it becomes a note in an emotional scale, and will never change.'

'Do you think', asked Pauline, 'that a great actor can get inside *any* character?'

'Within reasonable limits, yes. Actors are of two kinds: those who can play anything, and those who can play only themselves. The latter can charm, if their personalities are charming, but they are not, in the true sense, actors at all. For instance,' he said, turning to Dolores, 'I am told that you are just as good in the *Carrosse du Saint-Sacrement* as in *La Dame aux camélias*. If that is the case, then you are indeed a great actress.'

'But has not a woman the right', asked Lolita, with a deferential smile, 'to combine in her own life, La Périchole and Marguerite Gautier? A coquette may still be capable of true passion – though not with the same men, that is all, *no*?'

'She has intelligence,' murmured Bertrand Schmitt to Pauline.

'A great deal,' she replied with the pride and satisfaction of a professor lecturing on his special subject.

Then, Bertrand set about explaining that there are also two distinct types of novelist: those who write only about themselves, and those who can exhibit human-nature in many forms.

'I do not mean that the former are necessarily of a lower grade. Stendhal is a good example. He painted the man he was, the man he would have liked to be, the man he might have been had he been born the son of a banker; and, also, the woman he would have been if he had been a woman – and the woman, too, by whom he would have liked to be loved. Balzac, on the other hand, is an example of the creative novelist. As you were saying, Laurent, he can get under the skin of a moneylender, an old maid, a door-keeper, a conspirator, or a judge ...'

'But Balzac also makes use of himself,' objected Christian: 'For example, in *Louis Lambert*, in the *Duchesse de Langeais*, in *Le Lys dans la vallée*, and, indirectly, in *Baron Hulot* ...'

'Of course he does,' said Bertrand: 'Why should he exclude only himself from the *Comédie humaine*? Balzac observed his own reactions as he observed those of others, but not with greater intensity.'

Young Hervé Marcenat here intervened to speak of the 'point of real departure' which is as necessary for the novelist as the actor.

'Subjects, or characters, constructed on a substratum of some abstract idea, never – don't you agree? – wholly come off. Nothing can take the place of the inimitable irrationality of nature. The only thing I have against your admirable dramas, Monsieur Ménétrier, is the rather too large a part which you allow pure intelligence to play in them.'

'But I am not at all intelligent,' said Christian whom the last speaker had clearly annoyed. 'That is a reputation with which my enemies have saddled me.'

'As mine have me,' said Léon Laurent, angrily. 'Hostile critics are for ever flinging in my teeth the objection that I am an "intellectual" actor. That is not true. I never build up a character by a process of reasoning. I allow myself to become soaked in it. Some of the best actors I know are incapable of really understanding a word of their parts.'

'But does not the public notice that?'

'The public', said Jenny, 'never notices anything. A theatre audience lives in a dream, and, so long as the dream is not broken by some too shattering accident, is prepared to accept all it is given.'

'That is perfectly true,' said Léon Laurent. 'There is no limit to the power of the scenic illusion.'

'And that', said Bertrand Schmitt, 'is why it is so absurd to attach over-much importance to scenery and mounting. This modern mania is utterly nonsensical! Don't you agree?' he added, turning to Dolores.

'Oh! you must not ask me,' she said. 'I have come to Paris to learn, not to teach!'

'I am taking her tonight to *Le Chandelier*,' said Pauline. 'She will have an opportunity, there, of seeing an excess of scenic devices.'

After luncheon, Dolores had a talk with Léon Laurent, who promised to come to one of her performances: another with Hervé Marcenat, whom she supplied with all the necessary material for an article which Pauline had asked him to write on the Compagnie des Andes, and, finally, engaged Ménétrier in a discussion on the subject of *Viviane*. So animated did the duologue become that Claire rather anxiously drew near, and said, suddenly, with great determination: 'I am terribly sorry to interrupt you, Christian, but we are expected, you know, at three in the rue du Bac, and it will take us some time to get there.'

As always happens, the defection of one couple broke the magic circle. The other guests took their leave, saying they very much hoped that they would meet Dolores García again. Several of the men offered to give her a lift, but Pauline asked her to stay on.

The two women were left alone.

'And now,' said Dolores, 'we must have our little talk.' With a firm, but graceful gesture, she threw her cigarette into the fireplace.

'Let us not stay here,' said Pauline, 'but go to my own room.'

She led the way, and Dolores followed.

12

THE room was the one in which she worked. Dolores looked with curiosity at the stacked papers, the book-filled shelves, and, especially, at the photographs with which the walls were covered. She recognized Guillaume and Pauline in Egypt, in Rome, and, looking very much younger, in Toledo. They were depicted, younger still, in bathing-dresses on a beach.

'Yes,' said Pauline, dramatically, 'look well at all this, at twenty-five years of happiness now destroyed – by you!'

'Destroyed?' said Dolores sweetly. 'Surely, the victory is yours, since Guillaume has gone away so as not to have to see me.'

'The very fact that he took to his heels is a proof that he is not cured. Even if he were, things could never be the same again between us. I look at your far too lovely face, at your supple body, and then I think that *my* husband – it is horrible!'

Her lips were trembling. Dolores was visited by a perverse impulse.

'If I could really believe that I should always be between you, it would make me very proud. No! forget that I said that! It is the gypsy curse, and comes from part only of myself, the worst part! I do not wish you harm, Pauline: I never have. But how was I to know that your husband and you were a couple for whom love still counts more than anything? I had never seen you: I imagined that you were very much older than you are. Guillaume spoke of you with respect and affection, but he was certainly very forthcoming with me!'

'Petresco says that it was you –'

'What does *he* know about it? I admit that I wanted to make a conquest of your husband. I liked what he said; I liked his kindness, his simplicity, the child in him. I saw him as a man who might, perhaps, uproot me from a provincial existence. Yes, all that is true. But if I had felt in him a strong resistance, I should have led our friendship into very different channels!'

Pauline, with a violent movement, leaned towards her.

'You speak coldly, reasonably! Can't you see that, for me, he is the only person in the world who matters, the man for whom I have sacrificed everything? Then you turn up, you, who have everything; youth, beauty, genius, and take from me, without love, what I held as something more precious than life! You believe yourself to be pious, Dolores. I have seen you prostrate yourself on the stone floors of churches. After that theft, that crime, how can your conscience be clear? If you really believe that God absolves you –'

Dolores flung herself on her knees at Pauline's feet: her eyes were brimming with tears.

'But that is how things were! I say again that I knew nothing of you. You say *without love* – that is not true. I loved Guillaume through all those three weeks. You know, better than anyone, that he can inspire love.'

Pauline shrugged.

'He had scarcely started on his journey home than you, no doubt, deceived him with Castillo, while, all the time, writing him the most ardent letters.'

In an access of pain, Dolores shut her eyes.

'You are wrong, wrong! You understand nothing! Life has been kind to you, Pauline. For me, a poor girl, who has had to fight ever since she was a child, it has been different. Yes, I need men: I am compelled to submit to them no matter what they are like, but that does not alter the fact that for three weeks I loved Fontane. You will say – just another part for her! Perhaps, but I played it with emotion and with truth. I am very sensual; so is Guillaume ...'

'Oh! stop, stop!' cried Pauline, and started to sob.

Dolores was crying, too, and took her in her arms. After a while they both grew calmer, and Dolores laid her golden head on Pauline's lap, unconstrainedly, and with gentleness.

'It is so necessary to understand,' she murmured. 'You, Pauline, have chosen the respectable, the conventional way of life. You have devoted yourself to one man, and one only. In that you may have found great happiness – I do not know. But there is another way of living, a free, a passionate way, and that is the one I have chosen. It gives moments of wonderful happiness – but many, too, of rending despair. But is it – *cómo se dice?* – the less noble? I do not think so. You staked everything on security; I have been prepared to take risks. Ten times in my life I have plunged into the unknown: on the stage when, having won fame in classic tragedy, I suddenly asked to be allowed to be given my chance in realistic comedy: in my life of love, when I abandoned the powerful protector with whom my future was assured, for a poor and unknown actor whom I married. I swear to you that men adore such lack of prudence. They give themselves to women who know what it is to dare! Is that my fault?'

'I don't want you to think for a moment', said Pauline, 'that I, too, haven't taken risks. I was Guillaume's mistress before ever I became his wife, at a time when he did not want to get married.'

'Really? Oh! that *does* surprise me! I had thought of you as so very much a *bourgeoise*.'

She gazed up at Pauline, and there was something of exaltation in her eyes.

'I love you, Pauline; you believe that, *no*? I love you and I admire you. You are beautiful, *querida*; yes, you are beautiful: the most luminous brow in all the world, and such eloquent eyes. You are very brilliant; you know everything. Yesterday evening, after our drive round Paris, we talked of you, my friends and I: "That is a remarkable woman," we said. There is grandeur in your feelings, and, in that way, you are, I think, superior to Guillaume. No, let me go on: Guillaume says a great many very lovely things about love, but he is really a sensualist. It is the body that he has beside him at the moment that inspires those things in him. He knows nothing of – *cómo se dice?* – exclusive passion: but you, *querida* – '

'You met Guillaume late in his life,' said Pauline. 'I knew him when he was young and passionate. For twenty-five years, we have been perfectly at one, and wholly happy. And then, suddenly, those demons who haunt the evening of men's lives, took possession of him. I never believed in their existence, but now I see, only too clearly, how they can torment the ageing. And so, you see, I have lost him.'

Lolita got to her feet:

'You *have not* lost him, as you well know! Only, if you wish to keep him, you must be a little more skilful. Don't say no: there is nothing to be ashamed of in trying to defend one's love. You are still, for Guillaume, a perfect companion to him in his hours of work, but there is one side of him that you neglect. I know what I am talking of: intellectual women play a losing hand in the game of love. Men grow tired of women who wear them out mentally. Oh, yes, they enjoy talking with them, but a pretty, well-covered girl has only to come within range, for them to be after her like a shot. Yes, Pauline, that is so. *El hombre, en las mujeres, busca un poco de fiesta.* A man looks for a little gaiety in women – *cómo se dice?* – some relaxation. I used to make Guillaume laugh for hours.'

'We must not force our talents,' said Pauline: 'I should look a fool if I played the child. Either he must love me as I am, or all is over between us.'

'Why, of course, *querida*. But do you not see that what

213

is true on the one side, is true on the other? You must love him as *he* is, and I tell you that Guillaume is sensual, that he loves gaiety and poetry. You have poetry in you, Pauline, I am sure, but you – *cómo se dice?* – hide it under a bushel. One can say that, can't one?'

Pauline was unconsciously fondling the curly hair which once again was lying on her lap.

'And there is another thing,' went on Lolita. 'You can be hard, Pauline, very hard: I have seen that – especially in your letters. But that you must not be. Why be severe? By what right? No one knows what goes on in other people. We all have our faults. Why are you not more religious? You are surprised to find me pious because I am not chaste. Nevertheless, I am a Christian, more so than you. I try to have charity; yes, that is true. I have tried with you. You must try with Guillaume. He is an artist. What he demands in the woman who is *his* woman, is warmth of heart. All artists are egoists. They must be, to protect their work. If we want to keep them, we must be modest, we must give them the centre of the stage. That is why the actress who seduces the great artist, soon loses him, because she, too, is an artist and wants to have all the applause. I have expressed that very badly, *no?*'

Pauline for a moment seemed lost in thought:

'On the contrary, you have expressed it very well. Yes, it is quite possible that, as I have grown older, I have become sharp, impatient, dictatorial, with Guillaume. It is possible that I have not shown him enough tenderness. But if I caused him to suffer, why did he not say so?'

'They never do,' said Lolita, getting up and going to the glass to arrange her hair. 'They never speak, but sulk, and look elsewhere for their ration of happiness. It is for us to feel, for us to fight. You are foolish, Pauline, to let your hair go white, and always to dress in such gloomy colours.

You could make yourself look ten years younger.'

'But Guillaume likes black. Since we are talking intimately, you might like to know that he told me how, once in Lima, he criticized you for wearing a dress of too glaring a red.'

'I do not remember. It is possible. All the same, I am sure that when he remembers me, he thinks of me in gay colours – a sailor's jersey, with my hair all loose. Your grey wave, Pauline, is too perfect, too regular.'

She passed her fingers through Pauline's hair, slightly disarranged it, and gave her a friendly smile.

'I must be off to the theatre,' she said: 'I am expected. But I am glad to have had this talk with you. I think I love you, Pauline. I am your friend. I feel that I have known you always. You do believe me, *no?*'

Before parting, the two women embraced.

13

THE performances given in Paris by the Compagnie des Andes were a sad failure. The adjustments had been difficult. The scenery, made to fit other theatres, had puzzled the French stage-hands, with the result that the changes were too slow, and the intervals a great deal too long. Unaccustomed food had made the actors sluggish. Conchita first, and then Corinna, failed to turn up at rehearsal. In vain did Dolores try to infect the company with her own burning desire to conquer Paris. At the dress-rehearsal, the performers felt that the audience was not following what they said. They became discouraged, and the slackness of their playing paralysed even her.

Thanks to the influence of Madame Fontane, a few of the critics were loud in their praise: others treated with irreverent contempt a 'show' which, to them, was unintelligible. Only Hervé Marcenat analysed, as it deserved, the genius of Dolores García. He possessed powers of judgement which his colleagues lacked. As to the general public, it stayed away. The Spanish colony, deeply divided, was more interested in the politics of the actors than in their talents. The French members of the audience, except for a small group of hispanophils, did not understand the language. The final performances had to be cancelled, in order to avoid the necessity of playing to an empty house.

For Dolores García the disappointment was painful in the extreme. She had gone to Paris as a Mohammedan goes to Mecca, and Paris had failed to appreciate her. The realization that this was so was a bitter pill to swallow. For some days she tried to deceive herself with the hope that she might play in French. Pauline persuaded Léon Laurent to give the actress an audition, listen to her reading of the part of *Tessa*, and let her benefit from his advice. He succeeded in dissuading Dolores from making the attempt.

'You are', he told her, 'an excellent actress. I went to see your *Bodas de sangre*, which I already knew in translation. You moved me – and I'm pretty tough. But, though you speak our language well, you have an accent. Off the stage it is barely noticeable, and gives a certain charm to your speech, but it is an impossible handicap in the theatre, except in a very limited number of parts which might justify it. My advice, therefore, can be summed up in two sentences: spend two years perfecting your pronunciation, or, alternatively, give up all idea of acting in the French theatre.'

When Pauline tried to console her, Dolores said sadly:

'No: I cannot go back to school, and how, in any case, could I manage to live here all that time?'

'What will you do, then?'

'My old Spanish poet, whom I love devotedly, has asked me to go back to Toledo. He wants me to spend a month with him in his country house before returning to Lima. I have already been there. I like the country, which is sombre and mysterious. I shall accept the invitation.'

'Yet another moth about to burn its wings?' said Pauline.

Lolita had recovered her gay and vivid look:

'Do not waste your pity on him: he wants to be burned. He lives alone, so I shall not be hurting anybody.'

Next day, about noon, Pauline rang up the Hôtel Montalembert, only to be told that Madame García had flown that morning to Madrid. Very much surprised, she telephoned the theatre, but failed to find out anything more. The actress had vanished like a ghost.

Pauline heard nothing more about her, except for a half-crazed telephone message from Ramón de Martina who had been waiting for Lolita in Toledo, but in vain. Later, she was told by the young Chilian poet, that she had rejoined the Compagnie des Andes at Santander, without going again to Madrid, and had left Europe.

'She had been deeply wounded,' said Pablo Santo-Quevedo, 'and so, you see, she did not wish to see anybody.'

Pauline, much distressed, announced this sudden disappearance to her husband who was just terminating his Swiss tour. 'What a strange creature she is!' she wrote, 'to go away like that without saying good-bye, and without leaving a trace, like a phantom. She was, in the life of Paris, a will-o'-the-wisp which shines for a moment, dances, and then, suddenly vanishes. . . .'

14

Two days later, Guillaume Fontane was back at Neuilly. He felt pleased with himself, in a curious sort of way, for having conquered an almost irresistible temptation. Pauline's first comments astonished him. She praised Lolita endlessly, her charm, her intelligence, her virtues.

'Yes, Guillaume, I mean that: *her* virtues. Basically, she is an innocent. She has done me a great deal of good, as you will see. She has opened my eyes. Everything, now, is going to be different.'

They had left the garden behind them and had reached, without realizing where they were going, the bank of the small Lac de Saint-James. They had been walking fast. Pauline, full of her subject, told the whole story with enthusiasm, and without reticence. Guillaume listened to her with surprising readiness, partly because she was talking of Lolita, but chiefly because he had found again the Pauline who for so long had been lost. It was a beautiful autumn day. The water of the lake reflected a cloudless sky and motionless trees. He stopped, and raised his stick.

'I do not *want* everything to be different. I want to recover with you life as we knew it before these – hm – episodes.'

'So do I: but one cannot rub out a piece of the past, and, in any case, it would be a pity to do so. I have reached a point where I can accept the whole of that past, and even to love it. Yes, Guillaume, I am happy to think that you had that brief happiness – for you, for whom it will be a lovely memory; for myself, because I have learned to respect you. Yes, you have a right to my respect, Guillaume, in part because you have emerged as a conqueror, but, mainly, because you chose the path of renunciation.'

'And you, Pauline, for having got the better of your severity. What a joy it is for me to be alone with you again! Whatever its beauty, an emotion which forces a man to be divided can only destroy that beauty in the end – and himself with it.'

He stopped and stared at his wife for a long time as though he had only just discovered her.

'What the devil has happened to you, Pauline? You have grown younger!'

'That is another of Lolita's miracles. Haven't you noticed anything? No, of course you haven't, so I won't reveal our secret. There is only one favour, Guillaume, I would ask of you. Don't you think that, after all these years, you might stop addressing me as *vous*? That has always been my ambition, you know, but, in our early years, I felt in you a resistance which I could not overcome, and put it down to your persistent memory of Minnie. Later, I did not dare, and that went on for twenty years. But, since you accorded that favour to our charming friend . . . ? '

'But, of course, Pauline – from this very minute.'

'V*ous êtes très bon*,' she said. He corrected her gently:

'Tu *es très bon*. The only trouble is that people will be surprised.'

'People', she said, 'never notice anything.'

A young woman, very obviously pregnant, passed them with a soldier who was holding her hand. Pauline followed them with her eyes for a long while. She seemed to be happy and at peace.

'What a fool I have been,' thought Guillaume. 'Still, my folly may have saved us from a melancholy old age.'

Then he said aloud:

'*Si tu savais.* It is all really so simple: I was only look-
ing for – '
Their eyes met.
A swan glided by.

Some other Penguin books
are described on the
following pages